PRAISE FO

'A superb book in which tenderness, love and desire kindle each other into a conflagration of sexual rapture'—Bapsi Sidhwa

'Perumal Murugan opens up the layers of desire, longing, loss and fulfilment in a relationship with extraordinary sensitivity and surgical precision'—Ambai

'A fable about sexual passion and social norms, pleasure and the conventions of family and motherhood . . . A lovely rendering of the Tamil'—*Biblio*

'Perumal Murugan turns an intimate and crystalline gaze on a married couple in interior Tamil Nadu. It is a gaze that lays bare the intricacies of their story, culminating in a heart-wrenching denouement that allows no room for apathy . . . *One Part Woman* is a powerful and insightful rendering of an entire milieu which is certainly still in existence. [Murugan] handles myriad complexities with an enviable sophistication, creating an evocative, even haunting, work . . . Murugan's writing is taut and suspenseful . . . Aniruddhan Vasudevan's translation deserves mention—the language is crisp, retaining local flavour without jarring, and often lyrical'—*The Hindu Business Line*

'An evocative novel about a childless couple reminds us of the excellence of writing in Indian languages . . . This is a novel of many layers; of richly textured relationships; of raw and resonant dialogues and characters . . . Perumal Murugan's voice is distinct; it is the voice of writing in the Indian languages rich in characters, dialogues and locales that are unerringly drawn and intensely evocative. As the novel moves towards its inevitable climax, tragic yet redemptive, the reader shares in the anguish of the characters caught in a fate beyond their control. It is because a superb writer has drawn us adroitly into the lives of those far removed from our acquaintance'—*Indian Express*

'Murugan imbues the simple story of a young couple, deeply in love and anxious to have a child, with the complexities of convention, obligation and, ultimately, conviction . . . An engaging story' —*Time Out*

'*One Part Woman* has the distant romanticism of a gentler, slower, prettier world, but it is infused with a sense of immediacy . . . Murugan intricately examines the effect the pressure to have a child has on [the couple's] relationship . . . *One Part Woman* is beautifully rooted in its setting. Murugan delights in description and Aniruddhan translates it ably'—*Open*

PRAISE FOR PERUMAL MURUGAN

'Murugan's fictional villages are places full of quiet menace, where caste boundaries are protected with violence and social exclusion' —Ellen Barry, *New York Times*

'Versatile, sensitive to history and conscious of his responsibilities as a writer, Murugan is . . . the most accomplished of his generation of Tamil writers'—*Caravan*

'[A] great literary chronicler . . . Murugan is at the height of his creative powers'—*The Hindu*

'Murugan's insights about relationships spread throughout his work like flashes of lightning'—*Kalachuvadu*

PENGUIN BOOKS

A LONELY HARVEST

Perumal Murugan is the star of contemporary Tamil literature. An award-winning writer, poet and scholar, he has garnered both critical acclaim and commercial success for his vast array of work. Some of his novels have been translated into English to immense acclaim, including *Seasons of the Palm*, which was shortlisted for the Kiriyama Prize in 2005, and *One Part Woman*, his best-known work, which was shortlisted for the Crossword Award and won the prestigious ILF Samanvay Bhasha Samman in 2015.

Aniruddhan Vasudevan is a performer, writer, translator and PhD student in anthropology at the University of Texas, Austin. His much-lauded translation of Perumal Murugan's *One Part Woman* has become an award-winning bestseller.

a lonely harvest

PERUMAL MURUGAN

Translated from the Tamil by
Aniruddhan Vasudevan

PENGUIN BOOKS

An imprint of Penguin Random House

PENGUIN BOOKS

USA | Canada | UK | Ireland | Australia
New Zealand | India | South Africa | China

Penguin Books is part of the Penguin Random House group of companies
whose addresses can be found at global.penguinrandomhouse.com

Published by Penguin Random House India Pvt. Ltd
4th Floor, Capital Tower 1, MG Road,
Gurugram 122 002, Haryana, India

Penguin
Random House
India

First published in Tamil as Aalavaayan by Kalachuvadu Publications Pvt. Ltd,
Nagercoil 2014
First published in English in Penguin Books by Penguin Random House India 2018

10 9 8 7 6 5 4 3 2

This is a work of fiction. Names, characters, places and incidents are either the
product of the author's imagination or are used fictitiously and any resemblance
to any actual person, living or dead, events or locales is entirely coincidental.

ISBN 9780143428343

Typeset in Adobe Caslon Pro by Manipal Digital Systems, Manipal

Printed at Repro India Limited

www.penguin.co.in

MIX
Paper from
responsible sources
FSC® C047271

CONTENTS

AUTHOR'S PREFACE TO THE TAMIL EDITION

When the River Flowed

Many readers of *One Part Woman* (*Madhorubagan*) wondered what would happen to Kali at the end of the novel. Eager to see if I could respond to their queries, I wrote two sequels.

In *A Lonely Harvest* (*Aalavaayan*), I removed Kali from this world. I wanted to imagine how Ponna's world might expand or shrink as a consequence of this. I am unable to assess the extent to which I have succeeded in doing that. What I did not foresee was the increased significance the character of Seerayi, Ponna's mother-in-law, assumed in these novels. I became a spectator, relishing her talk, her actions and the ways in which she managed the matters that unfolded. I have taken the freedom to wander around inside the world of women.

When I wrote this novel, my writing hand moved with great ease. It was the time when the river flowed freely, tiding casually over hurdles and blocks, moving confidently towards the sea. Will I ever experience such a time again? Now my path is strewn with dams big and small. I might have to stay stagnant for a little while. Perhaps for a long time. I might even need another hand to help open the floodgates. For these reasons, this novel becomes very important to me.

This is the second edition of the novel. The reason I create identities for characters and the setting is to enable us to interact with them intimately. But I realize that these are times when all identities are being erased, or times when identities are constructed for particular purposes. I even wonder if we talk so much about identity precisely because of the helplessness we feel at its slipping away, at its loss. Therefore, I have made some changes to the first edition and turned this into an entirely fictional text. I want to let the world know that this is a novel, a piece of fiction, entirely a product of imagination. The words referring to sexuality, the events and the stories you find in this novel are all fictitious. I have created them because they are necessary for the novel's main storyline. Please read without any mental blocks. But if you experience any, avoid reading the book. That will be for your own good, and mine, and everyone's. Thank you.

Namakkal   Perumal Murugan
26 November 2016

TRANSLATOR'S NOTE

It has been my pleasure and privilege to translate Perumal Murugan's sequels to his celebrated Tamil novel *Madhorubagan*, which I translated to English some years ago. *One Part Woman* portrays the agrarian life of a loving young couple, Ponna and Kali, who are unable to conceive a child. The social expectations around marriage and childbirth and the couple's own intense longing for a child weigh heavily on them. Towards the end of the novel, we see Ponna going to a temple festival where, on one particular night, consensual union between any man and woman is sanctioned. She meets a man who—because custom accords him the status of a god for that one night—might help her get pregnant. The Tamil sequels *Aalavaayan* and *Ardhanaari* imagine two possible, alternative futures for Ponna—one as a widow after Kali's suicide, and the other a life with Kali, bearing his judgement, rejection and eloquent silence.

In *A Lonely Harvest* (*Aalavaayan*), we see Murugan detailing Ponna's life after Kali succeeds in committing suicide, unable to bear the thought that Ponna could have consented to being with another man, even if only for a night, even if only for the sake of a child and even if in a way sanctioned by custom. In this novel, we encounter Ponna's grief and confusion as well as the amazing ways in which solidarity, friendship and care operate among women. Her mother and mother-in-law close ranks around Ponna and do all they can to support her and protect her from the judgements of the world.

In *Trial by Silence* (*Ardhanaari*), Murugan imagines a different future, where Kali survives his suicide attempt but is unable to forgive Ponna or any of the others he holds responsible for ruining his marriage and life. Ponna is faced with Kali's incredible silence and withdrawal, his inability to even inhabit the same space as her. This novel, then, is a portrayal of the attempts at forgiveness, reconciliation and reclaiming of happiness and love.

I could not take 'Madhorubagan' simply to be the name of a deity and translate it as 'The Half-Female God', because the novel and its title are not about the deity in any significant sense. Despite its discussion of human attachments to divine forms, worship and practices, the novel is about the relationship between Kali and Ponna and their intense love for each other. It is about Kali's understanding that Ponna is an inseparable part of him—he is unable to imagine himself without her. And hence the intensity of his suffering when he sees her decision to go to the festival as a great betrayal of that oneness. Hence the poignance of his torment. Similarly, though at a superficially cultural level, the words 'Aalavaayan' and 'Ardhanaari' could be read as names of different forms of a deity, the novels have little to do with them. Translating them as such would have been misleading.

As someone who grew up in Tamil Nadu, and with caste and class backgrounds different from the one Murugan details in these novels, I am forever fascinated by both the familiar and the unfamiliar I find in his descriptions of people, land, food, customs, practices, animals, plants and so on. I have attempted to keep some balance of familiarity and distance alive in the translation. We find in these novels an agrarian world of a particular region in a not-so-distant past, with its social structures, relationships, values, possibilities and constraints. My focus has been on the tone, texture and feelings that rise up to meet us as we follow these richly imagined characters navigating their world.

It is not necessary to read *One Part Woman* in order to understand the sequels. Perumal Murugan's narrative beautifully catches you up with key aspects of the earlier novel's plot that animate and give force to these sequels and their imagination of alternative futures for the main characters.

I can only hope I am getting, at least, a little better at this work with every act of translation. And I hope you enjoy reading these novels.

Austin, Texas   Aniruddhan Vasudevan
19 September 2018

ONE

Ponnayi looked up at the portia tree. The day had dawned, gently caressing the leaves before scattering its light everywhere. In that early-morning glow, the tree showed itself in full splendour.

After Kali's death, the tree was the first thing that Ponna's eyes would fall upon as soon as she stepped out of the hut. And, as always, her gaze leapt towards that particular branch. It looked like a blunt stump—the stub of a severed arm poking out of a shoulder—with a round scar made by the saw that sliced it. That branch looked just like a limb that was growing and extending to a side. Earlier, when little boys climbed this tree, they always hung from this branch and moved along its length using both their hands alternately to hold on to it—first making their way to one end, and then back again. After that they would let go and jump down.

Like a lance held up, Kali would stand and stretch himself and, in just one leap, he'd get hold of that branch and dangle from it. Then he'd jump down. She used to make fun of him for that: 'It is just like they say. In a childless house, it is the old hag who does all the playing.'

That branch was Kali's favourite. 'Look how it stretches like a huge snake,' he'd say.

'Watch out, it might come slithering to bite you,' she'd reply.

But he remained steadfast in his affection for the tree. 'No matter how much you bother it, the tree will endure it all patiently. It is only humans who are unable to withstand even the smallest of troubles, my dear.'

True to his words, the tree had indeed withstood everything. It was *he* who couldn't. Somehow, she found it hard to see Kali and the tree as separate entities. That was why she was very clear the tree should not be felled.

Various people tried to persuade her to get rid of the tree. Even her mother-in-law said, 'The man himself is gone. What do you need the tree for when you have lost your husband!' Her father, standing by her and gently massaging her head, told her, 'When someone has died hanging from a tree, we shouldn't let that tree stand. It keeps asking for more and more sacrifices.' People also said, 'His spirit won't find peace in heaven. It will come and sit on this tree and just hover around here.'

But Ponna remained firm in her resolve. No one knew that her mind was suffused with memories of Kali climbing that portia. The cot that lay under that tree was a mere pile of ropes as far as everyone else was concerned—but for her it was the happy weave of all her times with him. In fact, she had not even wanted anyone to chop off that offending branch. But in the end she had to yield at least that much. Otherwise, she would have lost the entire tree.

Since this branch had a twin that had sprouted alongside it from the trunk before diverging and shooting up higher, they could not sever it too close to its base. They left a little bit of it intact. She took a stalk from the felled branch and planted it in a corner of the field. At dusk one day, she walked to the cremation grounds, her mother shouting and trailing behind, and fetched ashes from the burnt remains of Kali's pyre, and carried them back in the loose end of her sari. She put a handful of those ashes in the little pit in which she had planted the stalk; the rest she sprinkled all over the field. Her mother-in-law, Seerayi, who happened to see this, said, 'If you plant a tree in the memory of the dead man, is it going to bring him back? She has become insane! Isn't it enough that we have one portia tree tormenting us? Do we need to fill up the field with them?'

Then Seerayi pulled out the planted stalk and flung it aside. She sang . . .

If she plants a tree, if she plants a tree
Will the one who has died wake up and return in haste?
Will he say, 'I am Seerayi's son,' and bring warmth to my
heart?
If she plants a stalk, if she plants a stalk

Will the one who died get up and rush to us?
Will he say, 'I am Ponnayi's husband,' and bring us delight?

Seerayi broke into a dirge whenever she wanted. Even in the middle of the night, her voice rose in a cry that reached the entire village. Someone or other from the village paid her a visit the next day and comforted her. 'You can dissolve your sorrow only by singing it. It is not easy to cast out his image from your heart, is it?' Though Ponna was sometimes irritated by all this, she did not say anything. Hers was the sorrow of a wife who had lost her husband. Seerayi, on the other hand, was going through the twin sorrow of having first lost her husband and now the son she had raised so protectively.

On that fateful day, before the news reached Ponna and she rushed home, they had already cut off the rope from the tree, laid Kali's body on the cot and draped a white dhoti over it. Tearing herself away from so many people who tried to hold her back, she ran to the body, pulled away the dhoti and looked at the face of the man she loved. It was not Kali. Someone else. Someone she did not know. The eyes bulged out and looked at her menacingly. The teeth had closed hard on the tongue, which now protruded, bitten and stained with dried blood. The lips were chapped and swollen. The muscles on his face seemed to have slipped and slid from their places, giving his visage a misshapen appearance. Even his topknot had come undone. Never before had she seen anything as gory as that. She could not believe this was the face she had once desired and relished. 'Ayyo!' she screamed and fell in a faint.

A midwife was summoned to revive Ponna. By the time Ponna regained consciousness, it was time to take the body to the cremation ground. She screamed, asking the others to dig a pit in the field and bury Kali right there. But her brother, Muthu, said, 'Let us not do that, my dear. You'd keep thinking of him every time you go near the field.' She grabbed hold of both ends of the piece of cloth that was draped around his neck and punched him on this face and chest, wailing, 'You lost him! He was my everything . . . You won't live well . . . You won't live well!' Various people rushed to pull her away and free Muthu from her clutches. But her lament, 'You lost him, my everything!', kept rising up and thrashing against his chest. He stood rooted to the spot, like a tree, sobbing uncontrollably.

But no one respected her wishes, and the body was eventually taken to be cremated. Many people consoled her later, saying, 'He didn't live a full life and die in peace, did he? He won't be at peace in the ground. He has died young and strong. The good thing to do is to burn him.' But none of that gave her peace. Ponna recalled the portia stalk she had planted in the pit with Kali's ashes. Seerayi had already flung away the stalk, so Ponna then picked out a stone and planted it on top of the ashes in the pit. So what if they had cremated Kali? Did that mean they could cremate the memories of him as well? So what if Seerayi had pulled out and thrown away that stalk? It did not stop Ponna from constantly seeing his face in the rocks lying scattered all over the field.

Every time she went to the field, she looked at the stone. She addressed it and said, 'You have left me to suffer here. Is it fair? If you had as much as hinted at it, I would have ended my life. Why should you have died? What have you done? Why should you die? What did you do? It was I who ruined myself, all because I wanted to bear you a child. I talked to you about everything, but I failed to ask you about this. I allowed myself to be fooled by the words of others. I let them convince me that it was your wish too. My saami, my lord! You could have pushed me away. You used to tease me, saying that you would marry another woman. You could have done even that! Why did you have to die? Take me with you! Even if they chopped off the branch from which you hung, does the tree not have other branches? I will grab hold of your feet and go with you wherever you go.'

In those early days, someone or other was always shadowing her, knowing well that she would pursue such morbid thoughts in her grief. As a result, Ponna's own family members and Seerayi never left her alone even for a minute. Even when she went to the outfield to relieve herself, one of them came by and stood at a distance. At night, there was always somebody sleeping not far from Ponna. Her mother, Vallayi, said, 'It is all right to feel shame. But what was so terrible that he had to kill himself? There are women in this world who go after a different man every single day. And their husbands roam around, chests puffed out in great self-confidence. But I have not seen anyone like him.' All this talk was intended to comfort Ponna. But in her view, they had all planned it out and killed Kali and were now placing the blame on him.

Once the final rites were over, her father wanted to take her back to her parental home. Seerayi just cried quietly. Everyone else stayed silent. When Seerayi composed herself, she said, 'It is my fate that I should live and die alone. If she goes there with you, she can at least find some comfort looking at her brother's child. Please feel free to take her home with you.'

Some of Kali's kinsmen too supported the idea of Ponna going with her parents. 'She has no children to care for,' they said. 'From now on, all she has is her family of birth. In any case, that is the custom too.' But there were some others who said, 'What would she do for a living? Let her stay here doing what she can with the field and taking care of this old woman. This old woman too needs someone to care for her, doesn't she?'

By this time, some of Kali's kinsmen had begun to spread all sorts of rumours. There were whispers that she had had a long-standing affair with Sevathaan who owned the palm grove, that Kali had finally seen it for himself and *that* was why he decided to end his life. It was even said that it was Muthu who beat up Kali and hung him on the tree when Kali had confronted him. Some insinuated that Muthu had decided to usurp the property of the childless couple. Apparently, when Sevathaan himself was asked about all this, he neither agreed nor protested, but smiled meaningfully.

Learning of all this, Ponna felt no dilemma about where she ought to be. She felt that she would rather be nowhere at all. The right thing to do was to join Kali. What was the point of going on living in a world that did not have him any more? He was everything to her, but he was gone—he had not stopped to think about her for a second.

And so she just sat in one spot, crying. Her mother, Vallayi, had a difficult time coaxing Ponna to get up and eat even a morsel of food. Vallayi's constant entreaties seemed to make no difference to Ponna. The family was still debating where she should live thereafter, and so they decided to consult an astrologer. The family could only resume its worldly activities after the final rites had been carried out and they had paid a visit to the temple on the Karattur hill and prayed to the god and the goddess there. But during the intervening period of mourning, when it was believed that the departed soul had still not found peace, custom decreed that they could not go to the hill temple or even attend any auspicious events.

The big-moustached, elderly astrologer from Odakkaadu cast his tamarind seeds and read the charts, before saying clearly, 'I have confirmed this four times. The blockage is for three months. He was such a robust man. It is not possible for his spirit to calm down any sooner than that.

8

Calculate three months from the day of death. After that, go and pray at the hill temple. Then make offerings at our Mariyayi temple, and then do whatever you need to do.'

No one in the village ever went against that moustached old man's advice. But Ponna's father decided to also consult the shaman priest in Koonappalayam who was known for dancing in a trance. This priest did his divining work using erukkum flowers. He would pick up a handful of these flowers and cast them on the ground. He'd then make his predictions based on the flowers that stood upright and the ones that had toppled on their sides. He too declared that the period of obstacle would last three months. He also added, 'It was a life cut short. So it will keep returning with fury. Such entities calm down only after claiming another sacrifice. Please take good care of your daughter.'

So it turned out that Ponna had to stay put until this stipulated period was over. But she did not want to stay in the house. She preferred to stay in the farmstead. In a way, it turned out to be a good idea. All of them could stay right there and take care of the cattle and sheep. For those three months, her mother too stayed back with her. At first, Vallayi went into the village every day, to the house Seerayi had there, where she cooked food and brought it back to the barnyard. But gradually she started bringing the stuff one by one to the farmstead and did her cooking right there. As for Seerayi, she was always restless, and she had to be engaged in some activity or another. Ponna did nothing. She could not find her bearings. Her mother and mother-in-law did not let her out of their sight even for a minute.

She spent her time just sitting in some part of the hut. Being there felt to her like she was lying down with her head on Kali's lap or reclining on his chest. Now and then her gaze was drawn to that branch of the tree. It appeared to her in its earlier form, fully grown. At such moments, she saw a noose dangling from it. The very next moment, she would see Kali's body hanging there. She saw that gory image of him, the way she had seen him laid out on the cot, only now upright. His open tuft of hair would waft in the breeze. She could not bear to look at this for too long. It filled her with fear and rage, and she always started crying. More than the tragedy of Kali's death, Ponna felt that it was an even greater punishment to be left with that gruesome image of him. But seeing that frightful image day after day, she slowly got used to it, and even started talking to it.

Now, resolving not to look towards the tree any more, she took a pitcher of water and splashed it on her face. Then she brushed her teeth with some ash. And she felt a sharp acidic reflux rising up to her mouth.

It was this reflux that kept Ponna somewhat grounded.

TWO

Vallayi could not bear to look at Ponna in a white sari—a widow's attire. She was sniffling and crying, but away from Ponna's eyes. As for Seerayi, she was sad that her daughter-in-law's life too had turned out to be just like hers. She felt that at least she had had a son who had given her a hold on life after her husband died, whereas Ponna did not have even that. Ponna just lay on a cot, looking like a bundle of waste cloth. Or she sat leaning on a rock, looking up at the tree. Her mother would come to her with a bowl of food and wouldn't give up until Ponna had eaten something. If she were still a child, one could exercise some power over her and make her eat. But Ponna was a grown woman. How were they going to take care of her?

Had the two older women not been there, the calves and sheep would have been sorely neglected. Someone suggested selling off everything. Ponna's father and her brother, Muthu, decided to put it off until the period of mourning was over and their visit to the hill temple. Her father would come every other day and stay for the night. He would come after drinking some toddy. He'd look at Ponna and weep for a little while. Then he'd fall asleep. Every time he was there, he lamented, 'Dear girl, did I raise you so lovingly, did I carry you over my shoulders, only to see you end up in this state? You both lived so happily like Rathi and Mammudha, the goddess and god of love. Even though you did not have children, you were there for each other. But we all got together and destroyed even that. The entire village cast its evil eye upon a husband and wife who were so happy. My darling girl, you were happy as long as you were together. Just somehow spend your life in that memory. I will make sure you lack for nothing.'

Vallayi scolded him, 'This man does not know what to say to a child in sorrow. Be quiet, go sleep!'

Muthu came once every week. He hadn't spoken to Ponna since she had cried and punched him on the chest. Her voice and her words, 'You lost me my husband, my everything!', stayed ringing in his ears. He was tormented by the guilt that he was responsible for Kali's death. He had tried his best to ensure the plan's success without Kali getting wind of it. If only he had woken up early that morning, he would not have let Kali die. He would have done something to stop him. He was wracked with remorse for having slept off in intoxication that night, knowing that he could have saved Kali if only he had been a little more careful, that because of his mistake everything was ruined and Kali was dead. He had agreed to the plan only because he could not bear to look at the suffering the couple were going through because of being childless. Ponna was his sister. He loved her. But it was with Kali that he was really close. They had roamed around all the fields and hills. And Muthu could not bear to see Kali secluding himself in this farmstead. Now whenever Muthu visited here, he spoke a few words just to his mother and then went and lay down under the portia tree. Whether he actually slept or not, no one knew. He always woke up at the crack of dawn and left without bidding anyone farewell. He never showed his face to Ponna.

In the first month, some relative or another came over there to talk and spend a night. It was common practice in a house of bereavement for relatives to do that until things returned to normal. They'd try to dissolve their sorrows in talk. An old woman, who was like a paternal aunt to Seerayi, came over from Chinnur and spent three days there. She was over eighty years old, but except for a slightly hunched back, she was in fine health. She slept very lightly, like a hen. When she closed her eyes to sleep, her mouth would open, and she'd snore a bit. And then she'd be awake again the next second. She talked day and night non-stop. This old woman's visit became an opportunity for Seerayi to reminisce about her childhood.

The standard explanation given to everyone for Kali's suicide was childlessness. If anyone asked Seerayi about it, this was what she said: 'They didn't leave any prayer or offering undone in order to conceive a child. There was not an astrologer they didn't consult. None of the gods opened their benevolent eyes and looked upon them. *That* was what tormented him constantly. We had decided to wait for a year or two and then find him another woman to marry. On that day, he went to his mother-in-law's place. They had come and invited the young couple to the festival, saying that the deity would be going back uphill, that they were sacrificing a chicken, and he should partake of the feast. He had stopped going anywhere, especially because he was tired of people asking about their childlessness wherever he went. She too had stopped in the same way. But I felt that we needed to maintain at least some relations—if only so that someone would come to dispose of my body when I die. And so I would show up to at least pay respects to the dead even if I didn't go to all the auspicious events.

'As for him, he would only go to his in-laws' place. But he had stopped going there for two years, even for the chariot festival. His brother-in-law was a close childhood friend. Since he came over and almost begged him to go, saying, "How can you not come even to our place, Mapillai?" Kali decided to go to the festival this year. All right, so he went. Couldn't he have gone straight to their place? Instead, he stopped to look up his friends on the way. They are all boys from Karattur. He had gone along with them somewhere to drink arrack. He has a lot of friends, you see. As they kept chatting, at some point it became an argument. Apparently, one of those dogs said, "A man who can't manage to beget a child shouldn't open his mouth to talk here." Now, in these sorts of settings, it usually happens that some wretched dogs would say whatever they want. Why, even now, I hear that people are saying all sorts of things in places where they sit down to shit. Can we control dogs' mouths? It is natural for them to bark at the slightest noise. How can we live if we take all of it to heart?

'But in his drunken state, he even forgot about going to his mother-in-law's place afterwards and instead came straight here and sat dejected under the tree. I happened to come here at that time, because I thought I should feed the calves and clear out the dung since both Kali and Ponna were out of town. That's when I saw him sitting here and asked what happened. He didn't say a word at first. But after I pressed further, he told me what had happened. I said, "Oh, dear boy, everyone talks about us. It is as if we are here just so that they can have someone to talk about. What is new about this? Let it go. Intelligent men don't seem to be able to have children, but dumb ones seem to be reproducing in great numbers. It is all god's work, what do we know about it?" I comforted him in this way, and he listened. Then I said to him, "You go sleep, dear boy, I will take care of the cows." He said yes, and I trusted him. If I had sat right there and chatted with him a little longer, I would have read his mind. Why did I have to think about work just then! But I thought about work—and lost my boy!

'I was piling up cow dung there on that side, and here he hung himself. I could not see anything in the dark. He hung himself on this branch. It all happened in the blink of an eye. I thought I heard a rustle, and I came here to look. I couldn't find him. I went into the hut and called out his name, "Kaliyappa, Kaliyappa . . ." That's what I called him. We had named him after our family deity. So I always called him my calf, my gold, my god. I used to say that if one called out "Kaliyappa", it was as good as saying god's name a few times. But he didn't answer that day. I panicked, but even then I did not imagine he would do this. He was adamant, just like his father. Very bold. I thought he had perhaps gone out to drink again.

'This damned drinking habit was his undoing. He usually only drank toddy. He was not fond of arrack. He drank that stinking thing very rarely. I stepped out of the hut, thinking that perhaps he had gone out to drink again since this was the toddy season. If he did, then that meant he might go to his in-laws' place and eat some meat.

'It was then that I looked up—I had lowered my head at the threshold, you see. I saw legs dangling from the tree. I went running, crying, but I couldn't reach him. By the time I ran outside, screaming, and brought others, he was no more . . . Our people are scattered across the fields. Maybe if people were nearby and could have come sooner, we could have saved him. But his fate turned out to be different. Before leaving his body, god knows what his soul thought about, how it suffered . . . Did I raise him with so much care, carrying him over my chest and shoulders only to lose him so prematurely? I protected him from wind and rain, kept him safe from sun and toil, held him close to myself . . . And now he has left me all alone and gone!'

Seerayi repeated this, word for word, to anyone who asked about that night. Saying this over and over made her know it by heart. Among her listeners, it was only the old woman from Chinnur who dared to say, 'Seera, my girl, this is what you are saying, but do you know what the village is saying? They are saying, "The wife is an arrogant woman. She pushed him to it." They are saying she was having an affair with someone. They say all this within my earshot. For two weeks now, it seems this is all the talk in the market and everywhere.'

'You are twenty or thirty years older than me,' said Seerayi fiercely. 'Don't you know how the world makes up stories where none exist? Who really knows what is happening in other people's lives? It is true that my daughter-in-law is a headstrong woman. Just like him, she won't bear one hurtful word. While he would take everything to heart and brood quietly over it, she is different. She confronts the person openly. But otherwise, she is as good as gold, aaya. If anyone casts aspersions on her, their tongue will shrivel! How could she kill him and then go to her parents' house and sit eating in peace? Show me the ones who are talking such rubbish. I will whack them with a broomstick!'

Kali's maternal uncles and their families now became intimate with them again. The wives of both uncles had come to visit one day. Ponna never spoke to any of the visitors. If they spoke to her, she just listened, keeping her head lowered. Once, when she stepped outside to go pee, she heard the talk outside. Rakkasi, the wife of the younger uncle, said loudly, as if she really wanted Ponna to hear, 'Do our bad deeds leave us alone? It is god who decides how long a sheep's tail should be.' If Ponna had been in her element like before, she would have retorted, 'God has given sheep a short tail, but why has he given a buffalo a long one? So that it can use the tail to wallow in piss and shit and smear them on itself.' But now she came back in quietly, and wept. Addressing Kali in her mind, she said, 'Am I a woman of bad deeds? Tell me. Is it fair that you have left me alone to listen to all these words?' But when had he ever replied to her laments? He only ever smiled his crooked smile. That was all.

The reason for Rakkasi's anger at Ponna was something that had happened a while ago at the marketplace. Ponna had happened to run into her once at the fair. She was carrying twenty eggs to sell for six paise each. If she managed to sell them all, she'd get one rupee and twenty paise. She had anticipated that that would be sufficient money to spend at the fair. When Rakkasi realized that Ponna was looking to sell the eggs, she said, 'At our place, all the hens fell sick and died. We didn't get even a single egg. My father-in-law asked me to fetch some eggs from the market.' She was implying that Ponna should give her the eggs for free. If she had asked for the eggs directly,

Ponna would have given her four or five eggs. She would then have to cut down on her purchases. But Ponna did not like Rakkasi's coy sense of entitlement. So she said, 'It is six paise for each egg. You can take them for five paise each if you want.' Rakkasi's face fell.

Apparently, Rakkasi had said to everyone, 'It is not like they have heirs to pass on their wealth to. And she wouldn't give me even four eggs. One day, when she is old and ailing, who is going to care for her?' Ponna's response to that was, 'Who said we are heirless? If I cast some food on the roof, a thousand crows would come flying to eat it. Even her own children won't come to wipe off her shit, I tell you.' Rakkasi seemed to have held on to the grudge all this while, and was punishing Ponna for it now. Time seems to favour those who are cunning and conniving; it torments only the innocent.

Ponna's sister-in-law, Poovayi, visited one day. She didn't have much to say to the older women. She stayed with Ponna, slept next to her at night. It had been a long time since Ponna and Poovayi had a falling-out and stopped talking to each other. Whenever Ponna visited her parents, Poovayi would leave for her own parents' home. Some thoughtless word uttered sometime in the past had ended up creating this rift between them. When Poovayi was pregnant, Ponna had said to her, 'Tell me what you are craving for. I will make it for you.' Perhaps because Poovayi thought it would bring bad luck to eat snacks made by a woman who had married before her but was still childless, she said, 'No need. It is not as if I have no one to make things for me to eat. I have people in my family who'd do things for me.'

That made Ponna angry. She said, 'Who said you don't have people back home who'd make this for you? If you have everything there, why didn't you get pregnant there? Why did you come after my brother?' Ponna meant this teasingly, but her words stuck. No one got to know what Poovayi had said first. She said to everyone, 'All I told her was that people from my family would come with food packed for the way and take me back with them in a dignified manner. For that, she tells me, "Oh, so you only want the food from there? Why didn't you also get a child from your brothers?"' And everyone cursed Ponna, 'How could she say such unkind things to a woman who is carrying another life in her? If she had gone through that, she'd have known better.' Ponna retorted in protest, 'Yes, it is only *I* who talks here. She is mute, you see. She can't say anything.' And she fell silent.

It must have been seven or eight years since Poovayi had her son. Since then, she grew more responsible and patient. When she came to stay a night here, she spoke as a responsible woman. 'Ponna, see, whatever happened, happened. Your brother too seems to be wandering around listlessly there. All he does through the day is drink. When I said to him, "You have wrecked your sister's life. Do you plan to ruin mine too?" he started weeping. He cried, "What will I do if even you speak against me? I only wanted to do a good thing. Would I have agreed to the plan if I had even suspected this would happen?"'

Ponna reacted to this immediately: 'Is that why he sent you to me—to tell me what an honourable man he is?'

But her sister-in-law was not upset by this at all. Poovayi said, 'He told me, "She isn't talking even to me. If you go and speak to her, it might make her even angrier. Don't go." But I had to come. I won't speak ill of you. What is the point in apportioning blame now? Who thought this man would kill himself this way? A thousand things happen at festival time. If everyone reacted this way, there would be a thousand corpses every year. He was just so much in love with you. The problem was that it was too much love. Anyway, leave it. I can't take away your misery. Nor can I give you something to take its place. I just came here to tell you that you should now live the way you want. If you want to go there, to your parents', and live there, do it. Do not worry on my account, thinking of what I might say to that arrangement. I will only gain a companion if you come and live there. I will think that I now have another child who can play with my little boy.

'But if you think it is better to stay right here, do that. We will visit you now and then. We will never abandon you. Various people have eyes on your property. I don't have such agendas. I have only one child, and all that I pray for is another child to keep him company. That's what made me understand your struggle. Even though I have a child, I am still having to listen to people's cruel taunts.

They say, "She has been able to bear only one child." I can imagine the things they would have said about you. What we have is enough to pass on to the one child we have. We toil hard and earn the food we eat.

'If you want to spend time in both places, that's fine too. Don't give too much importance to what people say. Do what you feel is right for you. But never even think of ending your own life. Think of us too. Do you think we can ever be happy if we lose you too? I am already worried about your brother's behaviour. If you do something untoward, I dread to think how he would react. We would die every day just thinking of what you've done. Please don't put us in that position, Ponna.'

As Poovayi kept talking, Ponna's heart melted and she cried out, 'Nangai!' and placed her head on her sister-in-law's lap. Poovayi ran her fingers gently over Ponna's head in a gesture of comfort. It is in times of difficulty that we come to know who our true friends are. Hardship reveals to us our sources of support. It makes us appreciate the warmth of the fingers that caress us gently. It makes us realize the value of words. It bridges rifts. Poovayi had not spoken to Ponna in years. But now, it was from her that Ponna was receiving the kindness and consolation she could not get even from her own mother. From that day onwards, Ponna started thinking more about her brother. He could have told her that Kali was not aware of the plan. He had clearly felt that there was no way of making Kali agree to it. But it could have been done. They could have somehow got Kali's approval. And if they couldn't, they could have simply abandoned the whole idea.

She felt that not only Muthu, but her mother and mother-in-law too must have played their parts in that plot. She could not bring herself to fully forgive her brother. But he must be wracked with the guilt that he became responsible for the death of a man who was not only his close friend but also his brother-in-law. It was her mother and mother-in-law who had initiated the entire plan. Her elder brother simply ended up becoming a tool in their scheme. As she thought about this, all of her anger focused on those two women. After all their plotting and planning, now they spoke to visitors like they were innocent people. As people grow old, everything begins to seem casual and matter-of-fact to them. It is as though, having endured a lifetime of difficulties, everything simply becomes part of a routine narrative—and the heart acquires a numbness.

Kali's death has already become a story to them. Just listen to the way they narrate it to everyone who pays a visit. They recounted everything in great detail, right up to the fact of their going out to shit that morning. Seerayi was saying, 'The calf mooed at that odd hour. I felt a chill then.' None of that was true. It looked like they had turned a story into fact and had also started believing it. Vallayi too simply repeated that story verbatim. If Seerayi was not at home when visitors arrived, the job of narration fell to Vallayi. And she did her job perfectly, with not a word out of place. Only her voice was different. Looking at them both, Ponna felt sorry for her brother. So she told her sister-in-law to take good care of Muthu. Like Poovayi said, Ponna did not need to take on the sin of destroying another family.

It was true that Seerayi was the first one to see Kali hanging from the tree. But none of it happened the way she now told it.

THREE

For the people of the region, the Karattur chariot festival lasted three months. All the preparations were started right at the beginning of the month of Maasi, in mid-February. And the bustling shops and rides lasted till the months of Panguni or even Chithirai. But, strictly speaking, the festivities were only for twenty-two days. For most people, the twenty-third day was the day of the feast. In addition, the day the deity came down from the hillock as well as the day the deity returned were both important days of the festival. On those two nights, people throng to have a vision of the deities.

The crowds are greater on the day when the deities go back uphill than when they come down. People would gather in huge numbers right from the morning of that day. They'd come walking and in bullock carts. Entire families, entire neighbourhoods, entire villages would come together—a diverse array of all sorts of people. En route to the festival, there were water pandals everywhere. All the fields around the main residential part of Karattur lay fallow in that season. The bullock carts that came for the festival were parked all over these fields. It was considered a good deed to make one's field available for the festival. There was even a legend about a farmer who built a fence and refused to let his land be used during the festival; his stomach swelled up and he died on the last day of the festival. So now one couldn't see a fence anywhere in the vicinity. The saying was, 'Can any man think of fencing out god?' Those who owned wells kept them equipped with a rope and a pot. They also kept a large tub of water nearby. As the water level in the tub diminished, someone would invariably replenish it with water drawn from the well.

If you looked around, you'd wonder if it was a cattle fair in progress. People came with large parcels of food for the way. There were also shops that sold fresh meals. And several performances took place on all the four chariot streets and the pillared halls that were part of the temple in the village at the foot of the hillock. People could pick and choose the performance they wanted to watch. Those who wanted to see everything would spend a little time here, a little time there. At the pinnacle of the celebrations, all rules would be shattered. The night was its own witness. Darkness fell like a curtain over all faces. It is in such festive revelry that the primal man is awakened to life.

Since Kali refused to consider a second marriage for the sake of progeny, it was his mother who had suggested they send Ponna to the festival. But he did not agree to this.

Two years dragged on, after which they sent Ponna to the festival without Kali's consent—although they slyly made her think that she had her husband's consent. By the time Kali learnt about this, it was too late. He rushed back to his farmstead, distraught. He felt that everyone had schemed to betray him.

He could not accept the fact that Ponna went to the festival that night to be with a different man. Her life was intertwined with his. He could not bear to think of another man's scent spreading over her body. Her body had united with his. It had been lavished with his scent for twelve years. He felt that every inch of that body belonged to him. In some ways, he knew Ponna's body better than he knew even his own. He'd say her mouth had the fragrance of rose water, her armpits smelt of aloe vera, her bosom emanated the heady rawness of sheep milk and her breath carried the scent of the aavaram flower. He had understood her body as a bouquet of fragrances.

'And what about my way of speaking?' she would ask.

He'd reply, 'It smells of blood.'

That would make her angry. She'd weep, saying, 'You speak just like everyone else. Do I really speak like I am going to wound and gore?'

And he'd try to comfort her, 'Try frying sheep's blood. It has such fragrance! That's what I was referring to!'

He had been trying to mingle his own fragrance with each of the aromas of her body—and to turn both bodies into versions of one single scent. If a different smell impresses itself upon that body now, it would be a blemish—the kind of blemish that would never go away no matter what you do. He made up his mind firmly that his hands would not touch such a blemish. If it was true that all men became gods, then let that god enter and take over Kali's body too. What's the use of a god who has not paid heed to any of their prayers and offerings and has not entered his body?

Even though everyone said that many children in the village had been born this way, he simply could not come to terms with the idea. He thought that Ponna was his and his alone. That was why he felt hugely disappointed that Ponna went to the festival that night despite his wishes. He had expected her to refuse even if he himself had asked her to go to the festival. But she had gone all the same. Deciding that she needed to suffer lifelong for her decision, he tied a noose on the portia tree. He thought that his death would be an eternal punishment for her. She should think of him every day, and weep. She had to constantly repent for her mistake.

Kali did not sleep at all that night. Nor did Ponna. Nor did Seerayi, for that matter. She stayed in the farmstead until the moon was overhead. She was unable to fall asleep anywhere else but her own home. After arranging the second feed for the cattle, she got ready to leave for home, hoping she could finally get some sleep there.

Her lips kept chanting, 'Oh Devaatha, please bless my daughter-in-law.' She went home and lay tossing and turning on her cot. She might as well have stayed in the farmstead, because her mind kept wondering if someone would steal the chickens or take away the cattle and sheep. She also kept thinking of Ponna and fervently prayed, 'The good thing should happen.' Lips that prayed for the daughter-in-law somehow failed to remember the son. Perhaps that was what god couldn't tolerate. She did not even know that Kali had returned to the farmstead. Thinking that he was still at his father-in-law's place, she woke up very early, when it was still dark, and walked over to the enclosure. She needed to feed the cattle and clean out the cow dung. Usually, Kali did it. He'd have completed all the tasks before the day dawned. But she had taken this on because Kali was away.

As she neared the enclosure, she saw the thatched gate was open. And the dog was barking. Did a thief break in knowing no one was keeping watch here? If the cattle were gone, she'd have to put up with Kali's harsh words. 'Why couldn't you spend the night right here? What's there to be afraid of here? Why do you act like a scared young virgin?' He had given her clear instructions before he left yesterday. She had retorted, 'Go give these instructions to someone who knows nothing. I taught you all these things myself— and now you are trying to teach me?' He just cared so much about the cattle, the sheep and this field and enclosure.

In a panic, Seerayi ran inside and checked on the animals. They were all safe. She went into the hut. Everything was in its place. The dog came barking to her. She shushed it. She was certain she had shut the thatched gate properly when she had left, but maybe she had somehow forgotten to do that. These days she had a hard time remembering such things. As she chastised herself for being forgetful, she decided to clear out the cow dung before feeding the cattle. Since the dung pit was to the back of the enclosure, she carried and dumped the cow dung there.

The dog kept barking and running towards her. She shouted at it, 'What are you barking at? Can't you be quiet? It's dawn already, the sun will be up soon. You think thieves come at this hour? You are going to catch a thief?' But the dog did not relent. It ran in front of her, barking. Then it ran behind her, closing in as if it was going to drag her by the end of her sari, furiously yapping unabated. It was strange behaviour. 'Hey! Did you spot a snake or something? Why are you so agitated?' she said, and followed the dog. When she saw the dog baying at the portia tree, its gaze fixed overhead, she too looked up there—and saw a bright white dhoti.

At first, she could not make sense of anything. She wondered if the dhoti had been swept up by a wind and got caught in the branch. Then suddenly she realized that the dhoti was wrapped around a thick human body. She could not speak. Her voice came out in an incoherent blabber. It was only when the hanging body was turned around by the wind that she realized it was Kali. 'Ayyo! My god!' she wailed and ran outside to fetch someone. She saw some movement at a distance and hailed to them: 'Ayyo! Please come here! My god is hanging!' The entire village must have heard her wail. People came running. Kannaan climbed the tree carrying the sickle he found in the hut. He cut the rope along with part of the branch. He sensed that the person was dead.

Kali's tuft of hair had come undone, concealing the noose's knot at the back of his neck. Even though Kannaan knew there was little chance the person might still be alive, he had cut at the branch with great urgency. It was a heavy rope, made of big weaves, and was thicker than two hands could grasp. The sickle was not sharp enough for the task—it had already gone blunt cutting stalks of maize. Kannaan sat straddling the branch and forcefully aimed the sickle at the rope. He was agitated. As the rope slowly loosened, Kali's body began to descend. Raasaan and Sellan, who were standing below, got hold of Kali's legs and lowered him. It felt like bringing down something very heavy. And there was a strong stench that grew stronger as they lowered him further. But they did not pay much attention to it then. They laid him down, loosened the rope around his neck and placed their hands under his nose. Nothing. There was a little warmth over his chest. 'He has just died,' Sellan said.

As soon as she heard that, Seerayi screamed, 'My god! You have left me, just like your father did, you have left me alone and gone!' Two people held her and slowly moved her away from the body and out of the enclosure. Some who came closer to the body said, 'Ayyo!' and ran away. Someone shouted, 'Don't let any children see this.'

Kannaan, who climbed down from the tree, his legs still shaking, ran and shut the thatched gate and fastened it from the inside. But by then the news had spread and a crowd had gathered. In the body's struggle with death, it had ejected some shit—which is why Sellan and Raasaan now also stank of it. The penis was erect and was straining against the dhoti. Both men washed themselves with water from the wide-mouthed pot. They poured water over Kali and cleaned him, and brought a different dhoti to drape over him. But they could do nothing about the erect penis. All they could do was try to conceal it by piling more pieces of cloth over it. They could not loosen his hardened teeth and push the tongue back in. It was then that Periyasami said, 'There is nothing more horrific than looking at the face of someone who has hanged himself. Let us not show anyone the face. Cover it fully.' And so they did.

By then, Velu—who had run all the way across fields and hillocks with the news—reached Muthu's place in Adaiyur. Ponna, her father and mother had returned only around the time the rooster first started crowing, and they had just gone to bed after releasing the bullocks from the cart and tying them up in the barn. There was no one else at home. Kali had gone with Muthu to drink arrack, and so Ponna and her parents had gone to bed thinking that the two men would only return in the morning once the effect of the arrack wore off. Ponna's father, who was sleeping outside, woke up when he heard Velu shouting, 'Muthu, Muthu, dey! Your brother-in-law has hanged himself!'

He banged on the door. On hearing the news, Ponna immediately started running towards the farmstead. She didn't know what was going on in her mind then. She just ran.

Ponna ran all the way and stopped only when she reached the enclosure.

FOUR

After her sister-in-law's visit, Ponna seemed somewhat rejuvenated. She felt well enough to handle her own tasks. She arose before dawn and looked after the cows and calves first. She cleaned the plate she ate out of. She fetched her own jug of water to drink. Earlier, if any of the visitors approached her, she would just sit up in the same spot where she had been lying. The part of her sari that was draped over her chest would have fallen to a side. And she would sit there, her breasts visible, like old women sitting around without a care. She had completely lost her bearings, and people who came to talk to her would feel awkward. Her mother or mother-in-law would have to rush over and pull up her sari to cover her breasts. But she was not like that any more. She was careful about her sari, and even though she had not started combing her hair again, she did tie it up in a bun.

One morning, when the sun had risen till it was directly in her line of sight, Ponna's mother thought she could take a cow to the fields and let it graze there. And she thought she could perhaps persuade Ponna to go along with her. 'Ponna, do you want to go with me?' she asked. Ponna looked up, wordlessly inquiring: 'Where?' She had still not started speaking; she still couldn't find the words. Was this the same woman whose sharp tongue the entire village feared? When her mother told her where she was going, Ponna stood up and walked slowly behind the cow. It gave her mother some hope that her daughter might recover after all. Ponna felt like she was looking at her own field for the first time. Kali was everywhere. So many Kalis. Since the water level had dwindled in the well, he had been making sure that the coconut palms got at least enough water to wet their roots. He had dug a pit and a channel around the coconut trees to make sure that the rain water ran and collected in these pits and nourished the trees. From the curved etchings on the sand, she could tell that the rains that came after his death had indeed cooled the trees.

Two years ago, he had planted just one row of brinjal plants. There must be ten of them now. There was enough space between the plants for a person to pass through comfortably keeping their feet apart. Ponna had asked him, 'Maama, why are you planting them so far apart? So that the water we channel towards them might go waste in the sand between them?' All he said in response was, 'Just do as I say, my dear,' and went away to tether the bulls to the irrigation shaft. She yelled after him, 'Your mother might as well have given birth to a mute one!' And he retorted, 'I have married you so that you can talk for both of us.' She didn't say anything to that. She counted and planted the brinjal saplings. There were thirteen of them. Two of them were really tender and small. She was not sure they would thrive, but she did not want to throw them away, so she planted them anyway.

By the time she finished planting them, he had already drawn water from the well once and poured it into the channels. He knew that if he planted the saplings far from the well, the channel itself would consume all the water. So he'd had them planted close to the well. But still the channel would suck up three buckets of water. And the row of saplings would need three buckets of water. As Kali was going over this in his mind and was making the bulls draw water from the well, Ponna went over to him, untied his topknot and grabbed hold of his tuft of hair. The bulls stood arrested in mid-draw, and the empty bucket dangled halfway into the well. She tugged at his hair and said, 'What did you say? Did you say I talk too much? The village people might say that, relatives might say that, your mother could say that, my mother could say that, even alley dogs might say that, foxes could say that, but how could you!'

He leant his head back towards her in pain, but he was not ready to stop teasing her. 'So they are all allowed to speak the truth, and only I am supposed to lie?' He laughed. She gritted her teeth and said, 'So you say I am a chatterbox?' and gave a tight slap on his cheek. He said, 'Look! If you carry on like this, I won't keep quiet. I know how to respond.' Before she could say anything further, he quickly reached and grabbed her breast with his left hand. Her hands quickly let go of his hair and covered her bosom. In that little gap of freedom, he rushed and stood between the bulls.

His calloused, spade-like hands were always behaving this way. She used to say that she would have to cuff his hands when they went out. All those thirteen saplings they planted that day thrived and bore brinjals. It was only when the plants started growing that she realized it was a variety called 'cat's head brinjal'. It spread wide like rough hair on a dry head and took up a lot of space. Each brinjal was so big that it would easily feed a family of four. Ponna cooked whatever kinds of kuzhambu she could make with the brinjals. She proudly took some brinjals to her parents. But they were still left with a lot of them. So she went to the Tuesday markets just to sell the surplus brinjals. After the first year of the brinjal harvest, Kali carefully pruned the plants from the top and irrigated them again. They grew even more lush the next year. He sprinkled powdered cow dung under them and raked near the roots with a weeding stick. What a lot of effort he had put in!

Now the plants were in their third year. Without anyone to tend to them with care, they stood drooping. She sat down near the plants and said to her mother, 'You go tie up the cow in the field, Ma.' Running her eyes over Ponna and the well nearby, her mother rushed along with the cow. Ponna caressed the bristly stem of the brinjal plant. It felt like she was caressing his arms. She held the stem against her cheek. Definitely his hand. Suddenly, she removed the sari from her bosom and rubbed the stem over her breasts. His wide hands fondled her breasts. She thrust her chest forward in pleasure. She felt like she wanted more of this. She kept walking through the plants. How many hands did he have! Her mother came running. 'Girl! Have you gone mad!' She dragged Ponna away from the brinjal grove. Ponna burst into a sob, and beat her breasts as she cried, each punch falling hard and loud on herself. Her breasts were bruised. Her mother grabbed Ponna's hands and held them back. Weeping, she said, 'No, my dear, no, don't.'

As Ponna grew tired and slid to the ground, her mother held her in an embrace. Sitting down slowly, she placed Ponna's head on her lap. But Ponna could not stop sobbing. 'Your father named you Ponna, the golden one, because he wanted to take care of you like a precious ornament, but now you are bruised all over. Is this what we gave birth to you and raised you for!' And she wept, smacking herself on the head. Hearing this tumult, Ponna's mother-in-law came running there. Both the older women had been watchful about the fact that there was a well nearby. So Seerayi had panicked, wondering if something untoward had occurred. Now seeing them sitting close to the brinjal plants, she asked, 'What happened, sister?' Ponna's mother replied, 'See what your daughter-in-law has done to herself.

She walks in the middle of the brinjal plants and beats herself on the chest.' And she moved aside Ponna's sari and revealed her chest. There were drops of blood where the bristly stem and stalks of the brinjal plant had bruised her. There were a lot of scratches, and both breasts were swollen and bruised.

'Oh, you heartless man!' sobbed Seerayi, thinking of Kali. 'You went away in a second. How am I supposed to take care of her? Did you think about that? Did you think about what she was to you? I told you both not to behave like young newly-weds, that the world would cast its evil eye on you, didn't I?' Her sobs became uncontrollable.

She then walked over to the well, and from the water channel next to it, she plucked and brought some leaves of the coatbutton daisy. They hadn't had enough water, so they were faded and drooping. She took a handful, crushed them with both her hands, and let the juices flow over Ponna's chest. The redness vanished under the green of the plant juice. Ponna's mother rubbed and spread it all over her chest. It stung a little. Taking the rest of the coatbutton leaves with them, they both held and lifted Ponna up. But she stood up quickly of her own volition. She wiped away her tears with the end of her sari and draped it properly over her chest. By then, four or five people from nearby fields had arrived on the scene, hearing all the raised voices and commotion. Seerayi sent Ponna with her mother and stood back to explain the situation to the others in elaborate detail: 'He has gone, but I cannot bear to see her suffering.

She is not eating even a morsel. She has no strength left in her. Since she lay cooped up in the hut all the time, her mother brought her here on the pretext of taking the cow out to graze. And in the little time it took for her mother to tether the cow in the field and get back here, she fainted and fell next to the brinjal patch. You know how thorny the brinjal stalks are. Her chest is completely bruised.'

Ponna, who walked upright and unsupported next to her mother, said, 'Amma, go to our village and ask my brother to come first thing in the morning. We need to irrigate the brinjals.'

Her mother said, 'The water channels need to be dug out properly again, and the brinjal patch has grass and weed grown all over. How can we water that now? The man himself is gone, why worry about the brinjal he planted?'

Ponna spoke decisively, 'Look here. If you won't go, I will. Or else, I will bring the bulls myself and draw water from the well. Do you think I don't know how to lift water from the well and irrigate the channels? Your son-in-law has taught me everything. He taught me everything because he knew he would die before me.'

Ponna's hardened face and unflinching determination unsettled her mother.

FIVE

After insisting that her mother ought to go to their village and fetch Muthu, Ponna went to the field carrying a rake and a spade. She paid no attention to Seerayi's protestations.

'What strength do you think you have now? You ate nothing for two months. Listen to me. I will go and do the weeding. Please stay in for just a few more days,' Seerayi tried telling her several times with great concern.

But Ponna did not respond at all. The day before, Seerayi had fetched a bundle of grass for the milk cow. It had rained for two days, and lush grass had sprouted over the fields. The owners of those fields had said that people could feel free to go and take as much grass as they wanted. Looking at the groundnut fields made Seerayi wistful. She felt that if that idiot had not abandoned them and gone, their field too would have been lush with groundnut and maize crops.

Kali always grew some vegetables, chillies and other things in two small pieces of land, which made them some

41

extra cash. After all, there was nothing like having a man to work the field, was there? After her husband died, leaving her with a little child, what farming could Seerayi have done? It was only after Kali grew up that the field looked like a field. Now Ponna too would have to struggle alone. How was Ponna going to spend her life all alone? Seerayi spent more time thinking about Ponna than about Kali. The dead ones have no problems to face any longer; it's only the ones still left alive who do. For the one who dies, it is just the struggle of those last moments. But for the ones they leave behind, enduring each day becomes a big struggle. Yet she had to think of his struggle too. If all that one had to worry about was food, one could live like animals and somehow manage. But humans have so much more to worry about.

She cut the grass, deep in thought about these things. Once she had gathered enough grass to make a bundle she could carry, she noticed that some kalkumitti greens had grown here and there in the field too. It was easy enough to find regular kumitti greens, but kalkumitti was rare. One could spot it only when it flowered, but even then it would hide itself among other plants. One had to look carefully for it. That's what Seerayi did. She looked carefully and found and plucked some kalkumitti greens. There was a certain pleasure in looking for and finding something so rare. That night, Pavunayi Paatti from Vangadu visited them. She was like a mother-in-law to Seerayi in marital kin terms. Whenever Seerayi ran into her, Pavunayi Paatti was always in the habit of asking after everyone affectionately.

'Why did this stupid fellow act this way?' said Paatti. 'Even people who are starving manage to keep themselves alive somehow. Aren't there people who can only eat their daily meal if they work in the fields every day? So what if they were childless? Even in those days, my uncle was childless.' She went on to talk of the old days. 'He had three acres of fields. They worked hard and lived off that land for as long as they could. Later, they wrote off the land to the village temple. The land that belongs to the temple in my village today once belonged to my uncle. My mother had been hoping that the land would be bequeathed to her instead. But since my uncle had not been happy with my father's meddlesome behaviour, he gave the land to the temple. Nothing was ruined.'

The old woman seemed to know a lot of things. She kept on with her stories as she and Seerayi plucked the kalkumitti leaves from their stalks. These were tiny leaves that one had to pluck carefully. After plucking them, Seerayi wrapped them in a piece of wet cloth and kept them on top of the water tub. Then they dozed off, Paatti entertaining her with more stories. Paatti woke up and prepared to leave before dawn. She said, 'Everyone else goes to work in the fields. I am the only one who stays at home. I may not be of much help, but there must be someone at home, right? I take care of the house. I have never spent the night at anyone else's place. But ever since I heard that my husband's grand-aunt's grandson had killed himself, I felt that it was all right to pay a visit and stay the night. That's why I came at a late hour. But if I leave now I will reach home before the heat becomes severe. He is gone now—but those of you who are alive, please don't dwell on it forever. Live well . . . Ponna, dear girl, god gives us our life, and he takes it back when he wants to. We don't have the right to end it forcibly.' With that, Paatti drank a little water, and left.

Seerayi had asked Paatti to stay and eat some gruel and greens before leaving, but the old woman refused. So it was only after Paatti had left that Seerayi started mashing the kalkumitti greens. It had the fragrance of ghee. According to custom, she shouldn't use any seasoning until the period of mourning was over. Even a little seasoning would waft across the fields. Just when Seerayi was thinking of how the aroma of these leaves was making her forget her worries, she heard Ponna's voice from the field. It had become quite a task to bring Ponna back home and make her eat a little. Like a madwoman, Ponna kept saying to her mother, 'Why haven't you gone to the village yet? Go fetch my brother, go, go!' Seerayi tried comforting her. 'What has happened to you, Ponna? Let your mother eat a little gruel before she leaves. You only need help with irrigating the field once the sun is up. He will come. If not, I will draw water myself. Now eat.' She made Ponna eat a little gruel. Ponna was in no state to enjoy the kalkumitti greens. She just sat there, staring at the portia tree, and distractedly swallowed some morsels.

After that, she wiped her hands on the end of her sari, and set off again. Seerayi had not expected this sort of behaviour from her. Perhaps the field reignited the memories of Kali. All right, let her do as much work as she could. Seerayi went about her own tasks, keeping Ponna within eyeshot. Ponna first went to the brinjal patch. Once there, she did just as Kali would; she snapped the long stalks that had grown on top and threw them to a side. She plucked away dried and withered leaves and removed the brinjals that had shrivelled and become worm-ridden, and piled them all. Leaving intact the main stem below and the robust branches on top, she broke and cleared away everything else. Now the brinjal plants looked like Nallayyan Uncle's cropped head.

That unbidden image brought a faint smile to her lips. She was not sure if Uncle had visited after Kali's death. So many people kept coming and going. They stopped by to speak to her too. But she just stared blankly at them. None of their faces registered in her mind. She did not really hear any of their words. Perhaps Uncle too had visited. Kali had been close to him. But so what? Kali did not learn anything from him. What would Uncle have to say about what had transpired? Ponna pulled at the weeds that had spread on the water channel. The soil had not hardened. She could see the layer of grass that had grown close to the ground.

She dropped that task and went to the barnyard. She had tied a cloth over her head like women working in the fields always do. Seeing that gave Seerayi a little happiness. She took it as a sign that Ponna's spirits might slowly improve thereon. Ponna was very good at her tasks. In fact, she was an excellent worker. Keeping herself engaged in these responsibilities would drain away her sorrows. Ponna came to the enclosure, took some water in a little pitcher and drank it thirstily. It made Seerayi happy to see Ponna drinking water with so much eagerness. Ponna then took a basket, filled it up with dried cow dung from the pit, hoisted it on her head and set off again.

Seerayi kept looking at her to see if Ponna's gaze wandered towards the portia tree. It did look like she walked with her gaze fixed on that tree. Seerayi thought that all she had to do was change the focus of that gaze. But that might not mean much in itself. Ponna could still find other things that reminded her of Kali, and scream just like she did looking at the brinjal plants. They just have to be careful for a little longer. They really should have felled and removed that tree altogether. It just sat there and bore witness to everything. How many generations would it have seen? Ponna would never agree to have the tree removed—any attempt to do so was met with intense protests from her, as though chopping the tree was somehow akin to actually hurting her, chopping away at her very life. How she had screamed when they chopped down the branch from which he had hanged! Chinnaan, who came to do the chopping, had said, 'God! Her screams are giving me the shivers. Let's not do it.' But Ponna's father reasoned, 'She would suffer and scream more if that branch continued to be there. Try not to listen to her. Just do the job quickly and leave.' Using the sharp-edged saw he had brought,

Kannaan finished the job quickly. Seerayi now wondered when the entire tree would meet that fate.

On the pretext of herding the sheep to graze, Seerayi followed Ponna into the field. Ponna spread the dried cow dung over the plant bed and used the handle of the spade to break them down into smaller pieces. Then she used the rake to turn over the soil. It had hardened. In some places, she pushed in the rake forcefully. Had she done this after one round of watering, the soil would have turned over smoothly. But she had no patience for that. Even though she had little physical strength, she was strong mentally. Seerayi feared that Ponna might hurt herself with the thorny brinjal stalks again. Ponna kept at her task, wiping away her sweat with the loose end of her sari. The day grew hot. Seerayi wondered if she should ask Ponna to stop her work and come back in, but she was not sure if that was, in fact, the best thing to do. But, thankfully, Ponna's mother came back right then.

She walked up to the brinjal patch and said, 'Girl, you will fall sick if you do so much work suddenly after not doing any work for so long. Don't we have enough to worry about already? You have already done a lot. That's enough. Come. All that is left is to set right the water channels. We can get that done before your brother arrives and starts drawing water. Come.' Ponna quietly did as was told. She carried the basket with her but she hung the spade and rake from a branch of the palai tree nearby. That's where Kali used to hang them. The sapota tree was bursting with fruit.

Vallayi walked behind Ponna. On reaching the enclosure, Ponna washed her hands and feet and looked into the pots—they contained balls of hardened gruel. She took one ball, put it in a bowl and poured some kuzhambu over it. 'What is this? Nakkiri greens?' she asked.

'No, ma,' she was told. 'It is kalkumitti. Your mother-in-law found it in the groundnut fields and plucked some with great care.'

Ponna did not respond to that. She ate in silence, washed her hands, and went and lay down on the cot inside the hut. In just a little while, they could hear her steady breathing.

Vallayi came in quietly to check on her. Ponna was deep in sleep. When she realized how long it had been since Ponna had slept like this, her mother teared up. She felt that things would now be all right at last. Outside, she heard Seerayi bossing about the sheep. She ran out and hissed, 'Keep it down! Ponna is sleeping.' Seerayi lowered her voice and said, 'Oh really?'

Sunlight lanced through the gaps between the leaves of the portia tree and spread all over.

SIX

Since Ponna didn't sleep at night, Seerayi and Vallayi took turns staying awake, since they feared that Ponna might give them the slip and harm herself in some way. To help with staying up at night, the two women set aside some tasks that they could do. They took their time with laying out the feed for the cattle. Seerayi would say, 'Sister, I will take a quick nap. Don't you doze off too.' But how much sleep did they really manage to get at their age anyway? It felt like no time passed between closing their eyes and opening them. They let Ponna sleep inside the hut, and they lay on two cots right outside. The cots from Seerayi's house in the village had been brought over here to the enclosure. They needed an extra cot for visitors who sometimes stayed the night. Even if they heard a little rustle from inside the hut, they'd both quickly awaken and sit up. If Ponna walked outside at night, the dog followed her. And they followed the dog.

They both had a lot of things to share with each other. Seerayi addressed Ponna's father as her elder brother, and she considered Ponna's mother as her nangai, her sister-in-law. But she addressed her as 'akka', elder sister. They had never had any problems with each other, but only rarely did they get to talk to each other intimately. They had made up for that these past two months and had shared a lot with each other. Two years ago, on a night just like this one, Vallayi had visited here. Seerayi had sent for her. On that night, lying in the front veranda of the house, they had talked about taking Ponna to the festival. That had been the beginning of everything.

Now, on another night, Seerayi started by saying, 'Akka . . . why did we have to discuss that wretched business that night? If we had not started that, the two of them would have lived happily despite everything. Not only have we so unfairly lost a life now, we also have to keep watch over her day and night.'

Vallayi said, 'Her father too accuses me of the same thing. He even taunts, "If women get together and run the affairs of the family, could it ever go right?" These men won't do anything themselves, and they won't let us do anything either. We only wanted to do a good thing. Did it have to meet this fate? I can't stand to see Muthu's suffering, Seera. My daughter-in-law is saying, "It looks like you will manage to destroy my family too."'

'Akka, I explained it all very patiently to Kali. I told him that there were several people in the village who had done this. He didn't register any of it. Did I anticipate that he would act this way? What kind of mentality is that? What is it that Ponna has that no other woman has? He thought that Ponna should be his exclusively. There are women who quietly meet other men in the maize and millet fields, going there on the pretext of cutting grass. And later, they just wash themselves with a pitcher of water under a tap and quietly come back. We didn't ask Ponna to do anything of that sort, did we? All we asked him was to send her just once for this godly work, but it upset him so much. We should have done it without consulting him at all. But even then, there was no way of predicting what this stupid girl would tell him. She is in no way second to him,' Seerayi said, venting out her anger.

'That's not it, Seera,' said Vallayi. 'We shouldn't have let these two constantly be all over each other all the time. There are couples who beget children even before they start talking to each other properly. And they get to touch each other only under the cover of night! But these two? Were they like that? No. On that day of the festival, I did all I could to keep the two of them from talking to each other. But your son had planted a portia tree there, just like the one he had planted here. They lay under it, he saying sweet things to her, and she smiling at him. So dramatic! If we let them, they'd have had sex right then and there. And it was midday! That's where things went wrong. He did not want anyone else to have her. Even if it was going to be only once, he felt too much pride in letting his wife do it. What do you think, Seerayi?'

'You are absolutely right, akka. Apparently, in my mother's day, if you married a man and became a part of his family, you were expected to sleep with all the men in the house. My father used to call his father "anna", elder brother. I would wonder why he addressed his own father as an elder brother—so one day I asked him about this. He smiled and said, "Both of us have the same father." I was very young then. I could not understand it. It was only later, when I was a bit mature, that my grandmother explained it to me. She was ten years older than my grandfather. When my grandfather was five or six years old, they married my grandmother to him; she was fifteen. They were cross cousins—her mother was his father's sister. They had made this arrangement because they wanted to keep things within the same kin group. Apparently, the fifteen-year-old wife would walk around carrying her husband on her hip. At night, the boy would go sleep next to his mother. So what did my grandmother do? My grandfather's father would take her to bed with him.'

'Now things have changed,' said Vallayi, 'and are more civilized apparently. Our men crop their hair like white men, and even go to watch movies. That's what has led to all this nonsense. When these two visited our place once, the brothers-in-law arranged to go to the cinema in a bullock cart. They took their wives too! That too for the second show! They returned only at midnight. The next day, Ponna narrated the movie to me. The husband apparently beats up the wife because he doubts her character, and goes and shacks up with a prostitute. And the wife stays patient and tries to prove that she is a chaste woman. Have you heard such a story anywhere!'

'What the woman should have done,' said Seerayi, 'is, she should have said to him, "*You* went to the prostitute. And you thought *I* will sit around here staring at the roof?" And she should have whacked him around with a broomstick. Perhaps it was seeing all these stupid movies that made him so proud. Listen to this. You should have heard my grandmother talk about it laughingly. She'd say, "I was a little scared of my father-in-law, but how could I not go to him when he asked me to. He'd hold me close to his chest as if I was a little bird. I can't complain. He treated me well." My father was her first son. My grandfather was the father of that son only in name. After all, he was only six or seven years old at the time. Rather, my grandfather's father was the one who was actually my father's father . . . Those were such different times. Now people would laugh at us if we told them these stories. I asked my grandmother, "So when did you finally get to be with your husband?" She said laughing, "What could a boy who couldn't even hold his penis and pee properly do with me? It was I who taught him things once he was thirteen or fourteen years old." Grandmother died first. Grandfather lived much longer. I asked him too one day, "Thatha, I have heard that it was Paatti who taught you everything. Is that true?" He laughed, "Oh yes. Your grandmother was no ordinary woman. From eating to peeing to shitting, she was the one who taught me everything."'

Vallayi found it difficult to hold back her laughter at Seerayi's story. But she had to, because Ponna might be offended that the two old women were laughing and enjoying themselves in a house of mourning. So they spoke in low voices.

'In those days,' said Seerayi, 'people were guileless. They thought it was all right to do this—it was only once, after all. But things have changed today. You know Maachaami in our village? You know—that house beside that bald rock? Yes, that man. That man was conceived with god's help, you know. His father had no qualms telling everyone about it. He'd say, "Dey! All your children are born of humans. Mine is from God." Would anyone dare to say anything bad about god? There are men who beget ten children and pay no attention to any of them. They also call themselves men!'

Seerayi spat sharply, and then continued. 'Sadly, these two weren't like that. They fit together so well—like mortar and pestle. He'd wake up and leave from here in the middle of the night and come back home. And she'd be waiting for him there listlessly. If she went over to your place, he was unable to bear her absence for even a day. He'd follow her soon after. They had so much fun here in this enclosure! I never discouraged them, because I felt that they were young and should do as they pleased. But one night I happened to come by this place and ended up seeing them in an indelicate condition. I completely stopped coming here since then. All I did was subtly tell Ponna to be conscious of the people nearby. She is such an unpredictable one.

She did not say anything to me back then. But later one day she tells me, "Why don't you tell your son that?" I just said, "How can a mother go and tell her son something like that? Just be careful."'

'Nobody stopped them from living like that,' said Vallayi. 'Let them. See now, it feels like he has just died, but it has been two months. What did he take with him? This body either burns in fire or goes into the ground and gets eaten by worms. That's all it is. Why did he have to kill himself for this? If husbands had to die for their wives' faults, very many husbands would have had to die. If wives had to die for their husbands' mistakes, very many wives would have had to die. Why talk of others? How did you manage to live after your husband died, Seera?'

Realizing that Vallayi was casting a bait, Seera said, 'Why talk about all that now? I have lost my husband, I have lost my son—and here I am, good for nothing. I pray to god that if I am destined to have another birth, let him make me a crow or a sparrow. Human life is no small misery. Does any crow speak ill of another crow? Why are humans like this? Anyway, akka, why don't you catch a wink? I will go and take a look at the cows.'

Seerayi rose from the cot. They spent each night just like this, finding something or other to talk about. In this way, they managed to keep one eye on Ponna while also sharing things with each other.

As they exchanged these stories, so many of their own sorrows dissolved and vanished without a trace.

SEVEN

When Ponna woke up, it took her a little while to find her bearings. Vallayi, who had been lovingly watching her sleep, said, 'Ponna, are you up? If you want, sleep a little longer.' That was what Ponna's father used to say when she was a little girl. He wouldn't let anyone wake her up early. He'd say, 'You really get proper sleep only when you are a child. Let her sleep.' As soon as she'd hear him say that, she'd go back to sleep. Even now, she looked around confused for a few seconds and then lay down again. But she didn't sleep. She was now awake, but she just lay there, eyes closed. After a while she rose, went outside the hut and splashed water on her face.

She looked up at the sky. The sun had begun to slide down in the west. In panic, she asked her mother, 'Has Brother arrived?'

Vallayi said, 'He will be here soon. Do you want to drink the leftovers?'

Ponna nodded. When she went to the temple festival, she had been wearing a silk sari. It was a pale sandal-coloured one dotted with little floral patterns. Kali had bought her that sari. It was her favourite. She wore it very fondly. When she walked wearing that sari, a string of kanakambaram flowers on her head, she looked like a bride. Vallayi thought that she should cast out the evil eye as soon as Ponna returned. That was the sari that Ponna wore last. Now, looking at her in white, it felt like this was not the same Ponna. Sighing at this thought, Vallayi brought Ponna some watery pap in a bowl. After drinking that, Ponna rushed back to the field. Neither of the older women objected. Even if they did, Ponna was not going to listen. Also, if she worked there for a little while, she might sleep well at night just like she had slept that afternoon.

In the field, Ponna hitched up her sari conveniently, picked up the spade and started setting right the water channel. She was wearing a new white sari. If it got stained by the red dust of the soil, it would be very hard to wash it clean. She just alternated between the two saris she had been given during the rites. Seerayi thought that perhaps if she gave Ponna a few old saris, she could wear them while working in the field, but she was hesitant to bring that up with Ponna. Wearing a white sari took some getting used to. All stains stood out clearly on it, and they wouldn't go no matter how many times you washed it. They'd have to give it to the washerwoman and have the stains removed by

57

steaming. But if they did this even a few times, the fabric would be ruined.

Seerayi had separate sets of saris to wear for working in the field and for housework. There were always two clean and fresh ones lying about in the basket. She'd don them only if she was going out somewhere. And as soon as she returned, she would wash them, hang them to dry in the shade, fold them up and put them back as before in the basket. When she went out to work in the field, she wrapped either a torn piece of dhoti or a towel over her sari. She couldn't be as carefree as the women who wore coloured saris. Had she been so, she'd have to buy four new saris every year. And even that may not be enough. It would be a good idea now to ask anyone who went to the market to bring saris cut out of the rough, plain fabric. That would be the best thing to wear for work in the fields. Seerayi could not bear to look at the dirt from the water channel staining Ponna's sari. But she controlled herself from saying anything right then. She said to Vallayi, 'You keep an eye on her. I will take these sheep for a graze.' Then she proceeded to herd the sheep in front of her.

If she didn't control herself and just said what she felt like saying, people might think, 'She is more concerned about the sari getting stained than the fact that her son has died.' It is true that sometimes the mind valued certain things over actual people, as if those things would last us a lifetime. Even if Ponna did not react immediately, she'd surely take it to heart and bring it up another day. Whenever such a thing happened, Seerayi was left wonderstruck at how Ponna managed to remember all these things.

Four or five years ago, for instance, Ponna wore a new sari for the Pongal festival. Seerayi had asked, 'Is that sari from your parents?' Ponna just hmmed in reply. Some three or four months later, when they were talking about something else entirely, Ponna asked, 'That day, you asked me if the sari was from my parents. Did you ask that because you thought my parents don't have the money to gift me a sari or because you thought your son doesn't have the wherewithal to get me one?'

Stung, Seerayi replied haughtily, 'Oh my! Why do I care if it came from your parents or if your husband gifted it to you! All I need is a little piece of cloth to cover myself. I just asked casually. If I ask you anything again about whatever you wear, just smack me with that torn slipper.'

And Ponna retorted, 'Have I ever hit you with a slipper? Looks like that's the kind of thing you tell others about me. Once while sweeping the floor, it was you who flung the slipper at me as if by mistake. I would never do such a thing.'

Seerayi had, in fact, once wrapped one of Kali's old and torn slippers in a cloth and kept it in a corner. But since that was lying in the way while she swept the floor, she had picked it up and absent-mindedly flung it aside. However, the slipper had hit Ponna, who had been sitting on the raised porch, her legs dangling. Ponna had stored that moment away in her mind, only to later spring it on Seerayi, catching her unawares. It was precisely because of this habit of Ponna's that Seerayi had learnt to be careful about what she said to her.

Ponna worked as vigorously as a male worker in setting the water channel right. Since it had rained recently, grass covered the channel. It was not a very long channel—it only stretched about the length of one measure of land. But it looked like she'd cut more than one bundle of grass from it. As Ponna cut clumps of grass, Vallayi shook them free of sand and set the grass aside. There was no calmness in Ponna as she worked on the water channel; rather, she was fuelled by rage. Vallayi feared that Ponna might cut herself on the foot.

Muthu came as promised and went straight to the enclosure. It had been months since they had drawn water from the well using the bullocks. He brought the ropes needed for the job and dropped them in the drain channel. He did not say a word. Vallayi observed that he was not drunk. She said to Ponna softly, 'Your brother is here. He is now getting the picotah ready, see.' Ponna lifted her head to see the lever that would draw the water. The water channel was close to the brinjal patch. Kali had built the channel in such a way that as soon as it was flooded, the water flowed straight down to the brinjal bed. After removing all the grass, Ponna pressed down the soil to the sides, deepening the channel. She estimated that by the time Muthu drew water, she'd be done with this task.

Earlier that afternoon, Muthu was happy to hear from Vallayi that Ponna had sent for him herself. 'Really? Ponna asked for me?' he asked.

'Yes, my boy,' answered Vallayi. 'You should have seen her that day. She was like a demoness. I don't know what's going to come out of all this,' and described to Muthu what had happened in the brinjal patch the day before. '"Go fetch my brother right this minute," she said. She almost pushed me out right then to go home and get you.'

Muthu was amazed that she even called him her elder brother any more. He had thought she would sever all communication with him. After fixing the pulleys, he tied the water basket to the rope. The basket had been hanging from the palai tree. A squirrel had built its nest inside the basket. He picked up the nest gently and gazed at it. The squirrel had not had any little ones yet. He gently placed the nest in a nook on the tree where two branches met. He then fetched the bulls and secured them to the picotah.

The soil in the drain had hardened. When they drew water regularly, the soil was soft and ashen-looking. But now that they had not drawn any water for two months, it had hardened but it looked like they could still rake it and sow seeds. Muthu made the bulls walk up and down a few times without lifting the water in the basket. When the soil in the drain softened a bit, he drew just half a bucket of water first. Once the water dropped into the sluice, he stopped the bulls for a bit, rushed to the sluice and made sure the water stayed in by strengthening the edges with more soil. Then he took some water from this pit in a little pot and poured it down the channel. After he did that twice, the channel looked ready to handle more water. Thereafter, he cleared the bunds he had made in the sluice and let the water run. He then looked into the well. The water level was quite high. Groundwater had swelled after the rains. It had all stayed collected there since no one had drawn any water. There must have been at least twenty buckets of water in there. The brinjal bed needed only five or six. The bulls cooperated well and helped Muthu draw out the water.

After walking ahead of the bulls a little and lowering the basket into the well, he pressed on the rope twice. He could sense the rope moving, the basket tilting and getting filled with water. Then he pressed on the pulling rope and made the bulls move along. Once they walked half the distance into the channel, he quickly leapt and sat on the pulling rope. Now the bulls felt the weight balanced between the front and the back. The filled-up basket rose up and reached the sluice. As soon as he tugged at the tilting rope, the water flowed down. Seerayi came running with a pot. Before the water flowed out of the sluice and drained into the channel, she quickly dipped her pot into it and collected some water. Then as soon as the water started flowing out into the channel, she used the little pot to fill the tub nearby with water. If the tub was regularly replenished in this way, they'd have enough water for later. It was not an easy job drawing water from this well. If any of them tried to do the job alone, they would have barely managed to draw two pots of water. Their hands would have been very sore after that.

Whenever Kali had drawn water to irrigate a particular channel, he had used that as a chance to draw water for the hut and the enclosure as well and also filled the tubs. After his death, it was the two women, the in-laws, who drew some water by hand. It was the hardest of all the tasks. If they filled up both the vats, it would last them for two days. Now Vallayi too came running with two pots. Ponna was waiting for the water to come flowing down the channel—and it did, looking like little snakes moving, twining around each other. Ponna walked closer to the brinjal bed and scooped some water in her hand. It was red, mixed with the soil. She drank a mouthful, splashed some on her face. Kali was in the very water itself, smiling and saying, 'What is it, girl?' And she responded teasingly, 'Oh, so you deigned to speak a word to me. How very generous of you!'

With a quiet, steady smile, Kali flowed into the bed. Flattening down the soil that had been raked and piled, he slowly filled up the brinjal bed. He stood over the roots and sank into them. Ponna could not even hear Muthu shouting to ask if the bed was fully watered.

All that filled her eyes was the sight of Kali filling up the channel so completely that it looked like its banks would submerge.

EIGHT

'Shall I take these two bulls home with me?' Muthu said to Seerayi. 'How many things will you take care of here? I can always bring them here to work when you need them.'

She didn't say anything in response and instead quietly pointed at Ponna. But Muthu hesitated to talk to Ponna. And although she had listened to this exchange, Ponna did not say anything either.

Muthu spent a few minutes confused about what to do next, but then said, 'All right. Let them be here for now. We can see about it later,' and got ready to leave. Seerayi tried to stop him, saying, 'Spend the night here. Leave in the morning.' But he could not even think of staying in the barnyard where there was no Kali any more. It would be like lying down on a bed of thorns. Even worse was this silence from Ponna who once used to talk incessantly, like the patter of rain on a thatched roof. When even he could not accept Kali's death, how could she? 'No, Atthai,' he said, addressing her like he would address a paternal aunt. 'I have some work back home. I will come back after two or three days. Then we can water the brinjal bed again.' He turned and walked on briskly towards his village.

In the shed stood two bulls, a milch cow, a pregnant one and four heifers of various sizes—a total of eight. All of them were of the same breed—all offspring of the heifer Ponna had brought with her after her wedding. The animal had been pregnant when it first came here, and yielded a heifer calf within ten days of its arrival. Ponna let the calf drink plenty of milk and took good care of it. They only needed enough milk to make some curd for the house. Kali had been particular about curd—he never ate a single meal without it, and if it was even a little sour, he wouldn't eat it. He also didn't touch the curd if it was too watery and curdled. All he needed was good curd, nothing else. She made curd for him in different bowls. In the mornings, he'd mix them with the leftovers and drink up the blend.

Once she mixed some of the thick part from the curdled batch with the good curd, but he found out as soon as he tasted the first mouthful. 'What is this, my dear? There is no curd. You poured in the split curd, didn't you?'

'So you figured that out?' she responded. 'You should've been born in the priestly class. Then you could have eaten creamy curd for every meal. Not this broken curd. Maybe you let the cows graze on fresh grass yesterday. That is perhaps why the milk was a bit watery and the cream was not thick enough.'

He went ahead and drank it, saying, 'Even priestly classes get milk from us. Are we not fortunate enough to drink good creamy curd?' And as he wiped his mouth clean and got ready to go out, he added, 'Don't do this tomorrow. Then I will ask loudly so that the entire village can hear, "Whom are you saving for? Do we have children?" And you shouldn't get upset then.'

That made her angry. 'Say it!' she yelled. 'Try saying it! Call me a barren woman too if you want to. You have said it now, what does it matter if you say it tomorrow or not!'

He ran grinning as if he didn't hear her at all. Seeing him run away made her also smile.

He never added salt to the curd he ate. Referring to that particular habit, she once said to him, 'Only if you add salt will you learn some shame and pride. You just grin shamelessly no matter who says what. It could be your wife, or your mother, or any of the dogs in the village. Shameless fellow.'

He then explained, 'Try eating curd without salt. That's when you can really taste the curd. If you add salt, it is the salt you will taste. That's the taste of one thing mixing with another. We should also reject what the village people say just like we reject salt from curd. That's when we will know our own taste.'

She retorted, 'Then why do you mix rice and curd?'

He replied playfully, 'Hey, my dear! We should only mix things that can be mixed. Like you and I have mixed, see. If we mix things that shouldn't be mixed, that'd be like mating cows and goats. They will die!'

'No matter what we are actually talking about, you manage to bring up this topic!' she said with mock disgust.

Keeping Kali's fondness for curd in mind, she had made sure there was always a cow ready to be milked. Whatever was left after the needs of the calf and the house were met, she'd sell to anyone who asked for it. But all houses had cows. So there was enough milk for her to curdle and churn butter out of it the next day. If she went to Karattur once every ten or fifteen days, she could sell the butter in the Priests' Street market there. In the Tuesday market, they would buy it by weight.

Both the bullocks they now had had yielded two bulls at the same time. Kali had ensured their quality by checking the curl of the hair on their forehead. He raised them well, castrated them and used them as bullocks.

'In all these years, it is only now that I have got the right pair of bullocks. They work so well together. Whether they are working on the plough or at the well, they totally understand each other and move so well. And when I tie them to the cart, it moves like a palanquin. I should use them to fetch sand from the lake and spread it all over the field. It might even be a good idea to fetch four cartloads of manure from Karattur.' In this way he would often list his plans. He took great care of the bullocks. 'This is the good luck you brought with you, my dear. See how the cowshed is full, and so is the milk pot.'

And she'd say immediately, 'It is only my womb that is still empty.'

'That is all you have to say,' he would reply. 'From now on, when I am talking about happy things, you shouldn't say something that ruins it.'

Sridevi, that lucky heifer whom Ponna had brought with her, had died only last year. The cow had yielded one calf every year and filled up the cowshed. She had grown very old and was unable to even chew the millet feed because of the little twigs that would poke the inside of her mouth, making it bleed. Kali then started parsing out the maize stalks, cutting them into smaller pieces, and feeding Sridevi with care. He gathered soft grass for this old cow. He took care of her as if she was a little child. When she mooed in heat for a bull, he'd scold, 'You still want that. You can't even eat for your own body. Do you think you can nurture another life?' He didn't let her mate with a bull in her old age, but nevertheless, he was prompted to ask, 'How do these cows and sheep manage to give birth even when they are so old? Doesn't it stop like it does for us?' By then, he had spent several years with sheep and cattle, but it was only Sridevi who provoked that question from him.

Ponna had replied, 'Only if women give birth would you still keep them in the family. Only if sheep and cows give birth would you still keep them in the shed. Otherwise, you'd sell them for meat. That's why god has created it all this way. If women didn't stop being able to give birth after a certain age, wouldn't you men torment us?'

He said, 'All right then, you leave the house now. If cows don't yield calves, we sell them and get new ones, right? We can do the same with women too.'

'Sell this Sridevi,' she quipped. 'I will go with her.'

He couldn't say anything in response to that. One rainy morning, they saw the old cow lying dead. Kali mourned this death, saying, 'It had died quietly in the night so that we wouldn't have to witness and suffer over its death. Even humans are not so considerate.' When people came asking to buy meat from this cow, he refused. When someone said they could at least remove the skin and then bury the carcass, he didn't agree to that either. He said, 'This cow died working hard for us. Let it become manure to the same field,' and he dug a pit in the field and buried her right there.

When Sridevi died, all relatives came by to commiserate. Everyone from the village showed up too. For nearly a week, not much work got done in the field. The three of them spent their time telling Sridevi's story to all the visitors. When they told everyone what a fine breed of milk cow she was and how many calves she had yielded, people said, 'Please save me a calf from the next yield.' Many of them thought they could get a calf for free. Then there were others who thought they could get one for a pittance. Ponna did not speak much to the visitors. It was Kali and Seerayi who sang the cow's praises endlessly. 'Ever since she came here, Sridevi did not disappoint us even for a year. After yielding a calf, she'd be in heat again in just two months. And even when she got pregnant, she never stopped giving milk. Not a single calf wilted away. We'd stop milking her only when we noticed it was the kind of milk that came from pregnant cows. That's how much the cow gave us,' Seerayi said to everyone.

Had Ponna said the same thing, people would surely have remarked, 'God gave you a cow that never failed to yield a calf—couldn't he also have given you a child?' And that would have angered Ponna. In order to avoid such an exchange, Ponna just said a few words of welcome to the visitors and went away under the pretext of some work.

And now her brother was asking to take away the bullocks. With the bullocks gone, the cattle shed would look bereft. Just as the house had become an all-woman space after Kali's death, the cattle shed too would just have females if the bullocks were taken away. So she decided the bullocks would remain, no matter what. It was true that keeping them meant more expenses; they'd consume two pots of water and four bundles of cattle feed. But having the bullocks here was like having Kali here. Even if she thought he had gone away, she couldn't let him leave.

Ponna had resolved to keep him hostage in each and every little thing there.

NINE

Her mother and mother-in-law brought in the cows grazing in the field one by one and went about tethering them within the enclosure. Ponna could see it all from where she was seated. She could hear the sounds of the sleep being herded back. Birds were making a ruckus in the trees. One or two of them flew in and settled on the portia tree. They were crows. Kali might come even as a crow. His spirit was definitely hovering around here—and wouldn't be able to let go of everything so easily. He had always been so very fond of this enclosure. He could even tell, offhand, how many kovai on the creeper growing on the fence were ripe and how many were still new and unripe. How could someone who loved everything so much just drop it all and go away so easily?

There was no scale in the world that could measure the love he had for her. But he could express it. In a slight touch, in a single kiss. In just a single word, he'd manage to express the entirety of his affection. Where could he go bearing all that affection? He'd perhaps turn into a bird and sit on a branch of the portia tree and watch everything. He'd be in the gaze of the chameleon that moved on the fence. He could be glimpsed in the rebellious nods of the calf. His voice would be heard in the grunt of the sheep. He'd lie on the ground. His arms would reach out from within the brinjal patch. He had not gone anywhere. In fact, he was fully and completely right there.

Ponna was sitting on the flat stone that lay in front of the hut. He could be in that stone too. They had found that stone while ploughing the field. They had been sowing groundnuts. He drove the plough and she did the furrowing. As the plough moved along, pushing under the earth, suddenly its curved end got caught in something. The bullocks had to stop, as the ropes pulled them backwards with a jerk. He made the bullocks move back and tried to pull up the ploughshare from the ground. It wouldn't budge easily. It was stuck resolutely to something. No matter how hard he pulled, he couldn't draw it above the ground. He had to release the bullocks from the plough. The soil was wet, so he brought a spade and dug in a wide arc. The edge of the ploughshare was stuck inside a stone. At first he thought he could remove the stone and release the plough from it. But as he kept digging, he saw that the stone was a large one. He used a crowbar to pry away the plough from the stone. They were amazed at the size of the stone and wondered how it might have got there. They ploughed and sowed around it. But the very next day he went back to the field to turn the stone over. He dug around it and pulled up and rolled over the stone. It was broad like someone's chest. It looked wide like a ribcage. Once he rolled it over, it left a large pit on the ground. A person could stand inside it. Three could sit. He got down into the pit. It was just sand all the way down.

He said, 'I wonder if my ancestors have left some treasure here, but there seems to be nothing.' He laughed.

'Dig properly and look more carefully,' suggested Ponna. She thought there might be something hidden there.

Kali laughed and said, 'Let us show this to your brother tomorrow. We can offer him half of anything we find.'

He could not move the stone by himself. Ponna helped him. But it was still a difficult job. So he went and fetched Muthu that very afternoon. They used two crowbars, one on each side, prised the stone out of the ground and brought it all the way to the barnyard. They laid it in front of the hut, and secured it firmly in place with the necessary support on both sides. Three people could freely sit on it as if they were sitting on a veranda. One person could lie down on it comfortably. Muthu jumped into the pit and looked about thoroughly, but he could find nothing.

'We won't find any treasure in such a pit, Mapillai. It is where people stored grains in the olden days for safekeeping. Let us push some soil into it and close it up. Otherwise, some idiot might run and tell the authorities,' Muthu said.

73

'But we found nothing here,' reasoned Kali. 'So what if someone informed the revenue authorities? Are they going to behead us? Let them come and look at it if they want to.'

But Muthu scared him, saying, 'If you just lie about in the barnyard, how can you know what goes on in the world? Apparently, last year, they found a pit like this one in Kaikkaranoor. A kinsman who didn't like the fellow whose land the pit was in went and told the authorities that the man had found a pot of gold in it. The revenue officer came right away along with his retinue. And with them came a white man carrying a camera box. The owner of the land tried his best to explain, but the revenue officer simply wouldn't listen. The white man stood here and there and took photos from all angles. The entire village was terrorized by this. Apparently, only after the farmer fell at the white man's feet did the white man ask the revenue officer what the whole thing was about. And once the officer had explained the situation, the white man had laughed and said that they could not find anything in that pit because it was of the kind dug in olden days to store grain. And he asked them to leave the farmer alone. But the man had to still spend ten rupees to get rid of the officer and his retinue. Ten rupees is not a small amount, is it? The earnings from an entire harvest. We don't need that kind of trouble. Come, let us throw in some groundnuts into it and close the pit.'

And that's what Kali and Muthu had done. Kali had then washed the stone. It was black granite. Later, he had used a chisel to smoothen the rough parts of its surface.

Kali was definitely there in all these things. He wouldn't go away. Ponna sat thinking about him, when her mother called. There was some water boiling in the large copper vessel in the corner. Her mother asked her to have a wash. 'You have done so much work since morning. You will feel very sore later. Go wash yourself with some warm water,' she said. It was Kali who had made a little bathroom in a corner of the enclosure for Ponna. He had tied thatched screens together so that she could have a little privacy.

There was a priest family in Karattur to whom Ponna usually sold the butter she made. They had a little piece of land at the back of the house. An ancestor of theirs had had a good garden there sometime in the past. They had told Ponna that they wanted to have a garden there again. They needed help with getting the land ready, and also needed someone to bring the saplings and seeds to be planted there. When Ponna told Kali about this, he assured her that he would personally go and take care of it all.

It took him only three days. On the first day, he pulled out the weeds and got the place ready. The compound was nicely fenced in. The next day, he strategized where the saplings ought to be planted and accordingly dug out pits in all those places. He also dug out a water channel so that the garden could be irrigated by the water drawn from the well. On the third day, he planted the saplings and watered them. In one corner, he planted a drumstick stalk and covered its end with some cow dung. In another corner, he had dug a hole for a coconut tree. He put in a coconut and closed the hole. In the rest of the garden, he planted flowering plants and sowed seeds for the vegetables they preferred. The garden flourished in just a month's time. The owners were very satisfied. The woman of the house gave Kali ten rupees for that job. Kali took that money to Natesar, who had his jewellery shop in the same street, and got a pair of earrings made for Ponna. The earrings were shaped like mangoes. She proudly showed them off to everyone.

When Kali went to work in that piece of land, he always used the back entrance. There was a bathroom in that backyard. When he saw that, he decided he'd make one like that for Ponna within the farmstead. And so he had laid down four flat stones on the ground, and made sure the thatched panels were quite high and could conceal a person. Ponna could wash herself there even during the day. She had complained several times, 'What nuisance! I am not able to have a wash in private during the day even just to beat the heat. That's when some man or another comes by for this work or that, as if they could find no other time to drop by.' In the village, the women were in the habit of waiting till dark and then going to the back of the house to have a wash. If they were returning from a visit to a house of mourning, they'd go to the well, ask someone to draw and pour some water over them, while still clad in their saris. There was no way they could change their saris there. But this little bathroom was helpful to her even when she needed to pee during the day. Without it, there had been no place for her if she happened to have an upset stomach. She'd have had to run to the back of the house, trying not to hold the sari up too high, and draw some water from the well even to wash her hand and feet. She would irritably complain, 'I have to wait for darkness to descend before I can properly wash my private parts. But you men! You undo your loincloths and wash yourselves whenever you feel like it.'

This bathroom had put an end to all these troubles. It was a source of wonder for the people who visited the barnyard. Kali had even made a door to the bathroom using a thatched panel made of dried coconut fronds. None of this had really demanded any heavy labour on his part. Once, when there had been a mutton sale and he had gone to get some, he found two or three thatched panels on which the meat had been laid out. He took two of those with him and tied them together. He made them hold together firmly by using sturdy stalks from the portia tree and fastening them to the panels with fibre threads of palm sheaths. Then he fixed this panel in such a way that it would open just on one side—like a flap. He also put up a pole inside for her to hang her sari on. For a while after this bathroom was built, women who were coming from condolence visits would use it to have a wash and change. Ponna was very proud of that. But soon, water became an issue. Once, some five or six women showed up. All the water in the big tub she had kept inside the bathroom got used up.

After that, she made it clear to everyone: 'You are all welcome to use this bathroom. But make sure you draw one pot of water from the well and fill up the tub.' At this, people went away, muttering in displeasure.

Kali said, 'Poor women. Aren't we strong enough to draw and fill some four pots of water?'

Ponna replied, 'You know nothing, Maama. All these women come here and wash themselves happily. But then they go around telling people, "You should go and see the palace Kali has built for Ponna." Apparently, a woman in the cotton fields was singing the other day, "Her face doesn't wilt, her breasts don't sag, there you see Ponna, the wonder with a bathroom."'

Kali could not contain his laughter. 'Again,' he said, guffawing. 'I want to hear that again.' She came with a raised hand to smack him.

He leapt away just in time and quickly climbed up the portia tree. Sitting there, he sang, 'Her face like a flower that doesn't wilt, her vagina that does not droop, there you see Ponna, thanks to the great bathroom.'

Soon, more than ten bathrooms came up in the village. For a while, in the town square, men were heard complaining, 'Apparently, women too want an enclosure just like we have for the sheep and cows. That's when they can spread open their taps and water themselves. All thanks to this impotent fellow. He started all this.' After that, whenever any new bride moved into the village, the family got a thatched bathroom built.

Every single thing Ponna's gaze now landed on awakened some memory associated with Kali—and it filled her mind with him.

TEN

They cooked a kambu millet meal that day. Seerayi prepared it in a large pot, letting it simmer in a low heat and thicken. Vallayi cooked avarai lentils. When Ponna returned to the barnyard carrying water, Vallayi gave her some food on a plate. Had the period of mourning been over, they could have cooked rice. But that would have to wait until after they had paid a visit to the temple on the hillock. Starting to cook rice again would mean things were returning to their regular routine. Vallayi felt that Ponna deserved to eat rice after all that hard work she had done. She felt sad that Kali wasn't fortunate enough to live longer with a woman like Ponna who was so resourceful and worked so well in the fields.

Ponna, as usual, was running her fingers listlessly over the food on her plate. She was not able to taste or enjoy anything. She mechanically brought the food to her mouth and then swallowed it.

In an attempt to draw Ponna out of her private musings and bring her back to the present, Vallayi said, 'That is kambu meal and avarai lentils.'

Hearing that, Ponna shuddered and said, 'You made avarai lentils? Those are his favourite.'

Vallayi did not respond to that because she did not want to take the conversation in that direction. She was afraid that might take Ponna away from the good mood she had been in since morning. Ponna took a long time to finish her dinner. It had just started growing dark when Ponna started eating. She ate, one slow morsel after another, until the Karattur temple conch sounded sharply at eight o'clock. If Ponna were a child, Vallayi would have dealt her a few slaps and made her eat properly. But now she had no choice but to rein in her impatience and mutter under her breath. Even after washing her hands over the plate, Ponna just sat there. By then, Seerayi also returned after finishing her tasks in the shed. The two older women filled up their plates and sat down to eat on the cot laid outside the hut.

Vallayi said, 'Finally your daughter-in-law managed to eat a ladleful.'

The lantern inside the hut cast shadows, and thereby served to indicate Ponna's movements. She had gone and laid down on the cot. Vallayi got up in the middle of her dinner to reduce the lantern's flame. When Ponna sensed the light being turned down, she said, 'Don't cover up the moonlight. My maama loves that light.'

Vallayi walked out, shaken by Ponna's statements. She worried about what Ponna might do.

In the past two months, people in the village had started saying things. They were saying that Kali haunted at night, and they were terrified. He was a proud man. His spirit wouldn't calm down so quickly. When people die young, their spirits don't rest easily. Even during the day, fewer people now used the path between the village and the cremation grounds. Those farming families that lived closer to the cremation grounds now ended their workdays at dusk and returned home. They didn't even wake up in the night to feed the cattle. Many were saying that the sounds of ankle bells and a shrieking noise could be heard at night. Apparently, when Nachayi, who lived in a nearby field, went outside at night to pee, she saw Kali swinging wildly from a branch of the portia tree right in front of her. She ran back home terrified and then fell ill and was bedridden. Her family was now treating her with amulets and sacred ash. She also categorically said that she would step outside the house again only if that tree was felled and removed from that spot. So the very next day her husband brought the tree down and had it sold to the Karattur wood shop.

People started calling out to each other across the fields to make sure everyone was well and safe. At night, they lit bonfires and sat around it in groups. It was said that the shaman priest at Koonappalayam had proclaimed after one of his divination trances: 'There is a haunting in the village. At midday it will roam around as a fierce, swirling wind,

81

and at dusk it would bark like a dog. It resides in the portia tree. Be careful. It will go away in fifteen days, but only after doing one heinous act.' It was not only others in the village, but even Seerayi and Vallayi who had their fears. At night, if she heard the portia tree rustle in the wind, Vallayi would emit a sharp scream. But gradually, they got accustomed to these nocturnal sounds.

They both slept outside. If the cows that were tethered under the tree moved suddenly or if the branches swayed, Seerayi would sit up on her cot. Once, while she sat up after hearing such sounds, Seerayi said out loud, 'You are dead and gone. Now what have you come back for? You did not want us, you pushed us away. You did not listen to our advice. You are a big man, you know everything. We are ignorant folks, doing only what we can and trying to get by. Why have you come to see us now? If you move the branch, you think we will get scared and run away? Do you remember, when you were a little boy, I used to whack you with the ladle that I kindled porridge with? I still have that ladle. I have kept it inside the hut. Try getting any closer. Do you think I have grown old? I am still strong. My body might have grown weaker, but my mind is still strong. Did you think I was like you? What was the point in strengthening your body like a rock? What we need is a strong mind that is not assailed by anything. You wretched dog! You did not have what it takes to stay and live. You hung yourself. How did I give birth to someone like you?'

Vallayi too sat up, listening to Seerayi's tirade, and said, 'Yes, that's right. Ask him, ask your dear son that!'

Seerayi said, 'What is the point in asking him? If he were in front of us, we could shame him with our questions. Now he has become the wind, and wanders everywhere. How can we catch him and keep him in one spot?' Then she addressed the absent Kali again: 'As a young man too, all you did was roam around aimlessly. Did I ever ask you where you went and what you were up to? I know you have licked several cunts. But what a wonderful wife you got. She was at your beck and call. Has any jobless dog in the village said anything wrong about Ponna in all these years? You would return home late at night and knock on the door—after spending hours god knows where—and she would open it for you. You came at midnight for her, and she let you in several times. Sometimes you even came home at dawn, and she was still there, waiting to open the door for you. Has she ever been mad at you and slammed the door in your face? I used to wonder if that girl ever really slept or if she was always up, waiting for you. That's the kind of girl she is.'

'Really, Seerayi? Ponna has not said a word to me about any of this,' said Vallayi.

'How would she?' said Seerayi. 'She was so crazy about him. She is still crazy about him. If we let down our guard for just one day, she too would climb that tree . . . Stupid girl. He might have been her husband, but she should have still kept him within limits. Even when she came by here in the afternoon, they would go in and close the

83

door. Whenever she brought lunch here, it took forever for her to return to the village. I would worry about how she would walk back across the fields in the dark with all the creepy-crawlies about. Did he think I knew nothing about his behaviour? Had he stayed alive and dared to question me, I would have told him clearly: go and ask anyone in the village. Find out how many women kick their husbands out and bolt the door from the inside. There are several women who don't even let their husbands touch them. "You think you deserve me?" they ask their husbands. Ponna adjusted and accommodated to everything. How could you think of tormenting her? On the last day of the festival, she only went to see the deity. Not to sleep with another man. Did you go and see it for yourself? How did you come to that conclusion? What proof did you have? And even if she did go for that, she would only have been with god. You think you are greater than god? Had I known you would turn out to be this person, I'd have plucked away these breasts that fed you. You have ruined this girl's life. You think you will find peace in your death? No man who incurs the curse of a woman has ever found peace, let me tell you.'

Vallayi too spoke her mind. 'He keeps coming back here because he thinks he can take her with him. Why do you think the two of us are staying here? If we let you take her, then how can we ever call ourselves human beings? You think you can hover on the portia tree. We will chop it down. Not only this tree, we will also get rid of the tree you have planted back home. Then we'll see where you can climb. We agreed to marry our daughter to you because you were our son's friend. Have you any idea how lovingly we raised her? You think highly of yourself because you are the son-in-law? Respect is earned; we give respect only when you behave accordingly. Did we ever treat you badly? We never failed to invite you for Pongal and Deepavali—and we gave you the appropriate gifts and honour, didn't we? Did we not make sure that you could hold your head high in front of others? When the village said you were impotent, we said you could marry another girl to prove them all wrong. You didn't agree to it . . . We sent her there for just one day. What's wrong with that? Did she ever reject you? Look at her grieving for over two months now. She looks like she is losing her mind, she laughs for no reason. We don't know what is going to happen to her. She is so crazy about you. How could you leave her and go away?'

The branches of the portia tree stopped swaying. The cows were sleeping peacefully. It was quiet all around.

'Do you see?' said Seerayi. 'I think he ran away after the two of us united against him. But we should be careful. He might return in the middle of the night. Once he starts thinking of her, it does not matter what time of the day or night it is.'

Vallayi replied, 'Let him come, we will deal with him.' She picked up a broomstick and kept it nearby.

A sudden gust of roaring, laughing wind swept past them.

ELEVEN

Kali did come looking for Ponna. He paid no heed whatsoever to his mother's admonitions. Perhaps he never heard anything she said. He leapt from one portia tree to another in the village and finally arrived at the one that was in the barnyard. The cows and bulls recognized him. The dog too could sense his presence. They rejoiced at this familiar fragrance in the air. He caressed them and spoke to them. He stood beside the bullocks for quite a while. They stood staring at him, refusing to lie down like they normally did. Seerayi noticed that and scolded them, 'Why are you still standing about? Was the feed not enough? He has really spoilt you. Where else has it ever happened that someone actually fed every mouthful to his bulls as if they were his children?' And she pushed some vegetable refuse their way. But they did not eat that at all. They just stood there, their tongues peeking out and then going back into their mouths.

Kali stood stretching out his hand towards them so that they could lick it. He gently massaged their horns as they lowered their heads to lick his hand, and he said, 'Looks like Ponna has said she won't let go of you.' The dog brushed against him lovingly, curling its tail. It brought its mouth closer to his face. He pushed it away playfully. It stood at a little distance and kept watching him. The hens and roosters made restless noises. Afraid that they might rouse Seerayi, he waved his hand at them and shushed them. They quietened down and perched silently on the tree. It looked like he was happy Ponna had decided to stay right there in the barnyard. It meant that she too was fond of the place. Even though he knew she wouldn't panic, he felt a little hesitant to go and look at her face. He haltingly entered the hut. The cat leapt out of his way and ran into the alley nearby. He smiled, looking at his mother, and thought to himself that Muniyan's arrack had perhaps been a little too strong and pungent that day. Seerayi had drifted off to sleep as soon as she lay down. Thinking she was still awake, Vallayi asked her something. When she got no response, she lay down, muttering, 'You went off to sleep even as we were talking.'

The lantern cast a yellow glow all over the inside of the hut. Usually, they would put it out soon after supper so that they could save on kerosene. But Ponna had kept it burning today. In that light, Kali appeared as a large shadow. Ponna lay there, holding some brinjal stalks close to her chest. Thinking of them as his thick fingers, she caressed them distractedly, as if by reflex. Her eyes were closed, but she was not asleep. Perhaps she knew he would come. Her face looked wilted, just the way a flower of the portia tree would wilt, its edges growing redder and redder. Her lips were moving, muttering something. He stood there, wondering how to touch her. Perhaps he could gently move the strands of hair that had fallen over her forehead. Or could he touch her earlobes? She'd recognize him even if he gently blew near her ears. She'd know even the touch of a single finger. Had the situation been different, had he been alive, he would lift her hands and place them over his chest, then on his cheeks. Sometimes he would place his hands on her breasts when she least expected him to, and she would say, 'Your eyes are always staring here. You never look at my face while you are talking to me.' And he would say, 'When you see a spring, don't you feel like taking a handful and drinking to your heart's content! But okay, I will look at your face from now on when I talk to you.' And he'd kiss her on her face.

But today he did not know how to touch her. He was unsure, and he shivered a little. But if he just stood there doing nothing, he might lose the time he had. He might have to leave without letting her know what he came to tell her. That wilted face he saw in the light of the kerosene lamp, he realized, was alive with memories of him. The loose end of Ponna's white sari dangled from the cot. He held that end in his hand, and sighed. Then he touched her feet that stretched out from under the sari; they were stained with the dust of red soil. Perhaps she was feeling cold or because she sensed his touch, she drew her feet in quickly. But he did not pull his hand away. He could hear her whimpering. He too began to cry. He placed his head on her feet and cried. He kissed her firmly on the middle of her feet.

He pulled her blanket in such a way that her feet could rest on it and not on the coarse ropes of the cot, which might leave their rough impression on her feet. Now he grew bolder and took her hands and placed them on his chest. The palms of her hand had withered like a dried leaf. He then lifted both her hands and placed them on his cheeks. Her palms grew wet from the tears on his face. Her hands, of their own accord, wiped away his tears. He sat down and placed his face on hers. She moved and made space for him on the cot. This cot had been custom-made for them by the carpenter in Aniyur when they got married. He had made the legs of this cot with wood from the flame of the forest; they were strong and resilient to moisture. The frame was made of neem wood. The rope was made of aloe fibre, and it was relatively gentle on the back. The knots were close and tight. Two people could comfortably sleep on this cot, with enough space to toss and turn. Kali had taken his bullock cart to fetch this cot from the carpenter's shop. This cot was the first place where she lay down in his house. But he did not lie down next to her now.

Sitting beside her, he gently turned her face towards him and kissed her on the lips. To let him know that she had not fully made peace with him yet, she pursed her lips tightly. He tried to use his lips to make her relent. He then used his teeth to draw her lips out. But she was not about to let go so easily. When she realized he was stronger, she used her hands to push his face away.

'Why, dear?' he said pleadingly.

'You are sticking out your swollen tongue,' she mumbled in response.

He said, 'You mean, like this?' and stuck out his tongue and bit it down with his teeth. His eyes bulged, his face got twisted.

'Ayyo!' She shuddered and spread open her hands to cover his face completely.

Trying to move her hands, he said, 'Look here.'

'I am scared. Don't come near me. Go away,' she said.

He laughed and said, 'Look here, don't worry. I was just trying to scare you.'

He would often act like a playful child. If he saw from a distance that Ponna was coming to the barnyard, he'd go and hide. Once, he climbed up and sat on the portia tree. She arrived at the barnyard, calling out, 'Maama, Maama . . .' but got no response. And she could not find him anywhere. 'Where did he go?' she muttered and looked for him everywhere in the barnyard. When she was passing by right under the tree, he shook the branch and jumped down, shouting. It terrified her, and she screamed. She then said to him, 'We are familiar with ghosts in tamarind trees; you are a ghost in the portia tree.' One night, when there was plenty of moonlight, she brought him food.

A similar thing happened. She looked for him everywhere and then decided that he must have gone to fetch some palm toddy. It looked like all the day's tasks at the barnyard had been completed properly. She went into the hut with the dish she was carrying. Then she felt something brush against her waist. She turned around quickly, but there was nothing there. She thought she must have imagined it and set down the dish. Now she clearly felt something poking her waist. She spun around, wondering if it was a snake or something worse. She found nothing, but was unnerved by the entire experience.

The next time something brushed against her waist, she did not turn around, but only looked out of the corner of her eye. She saw a stick poking out of a woven basket and moving towards her. Having deduced what was happening, she calmly picked up the ladle that was nearby. Then moving swiftly, she pushed the basket and dealt several blows with the ladle, yelling, 'It is a snake!' Kali then shouted, bearing her blows, 'No, dear one, no, no!'

He was always playful like that. Once, when she was least expecting it, he came running towards her from behind the hut, his arms wide, and startled her with a highly demonstrative embrace. Yet another time, he sat hidden among the sheep and suddenly leapt up to surprise her. 'Don't do such things,' she said angrily. 'It scares me, especially when we are alone here.' He replied, 'Who else is going to come here? Not even a little insect can touch you without my permission, my dear.'

Is that what was happening now? Was he playing with her now, teasing her with his tongue?

She said to him, 'You hung from the portia tree's branch. Were you holding on to the branch with one hand?'

'Hmm,' he murmured. 'Did it scare you?'

'Of course it did,' she said. 'Who does things like that? My heart skipped a beat. There you were, with bulging eyeballs like a sheep's!'

'It is all a game.'

'But such games can turn dangerous. Tell me you won't do such things any more.'

'I won't. I won't do anything you don't approve of.'

'Really?'

'Really. I swear on your life. All right, now show me your lips.'

'Go away. You will bite them just the way you were biting your tongue.'

'I won't bite them. I just want to touch them.'

Slowly, she parted her lips. He pressed his lips on hers.

'Why is there blood on your teeth?' she asked.

'It's nothing. It is all your imagination. Now be a good girl and close your eyes. My touch is the only thing you will feel. All right?'

'You didn't care about me all these days. Now suddenly here you are.'

'I have been coming every day,' he said, 'but you never lifted your head and looked at me. I thought you were very angry, so I stood around for a while and left. But today you held the scales of the brinjal stalk fondly against you and called out to me. So I came.' Picking up the brinjal stalks, he threw them aside, and placed his hand on her chest.

'Go away!' She smiled. 'What have you come for now?'

'I am going to give you the thing you want.'

'Do you know what I want?'

'I have been with you for twelve years. Don't you think I know that much?'

'Will you be with me in the future too?'

'I am going to be with you.'

He buried his face in her. Now he did not need his own space on the cot. Kali spent a long time with Ponna that night.

When Seerayi woke up from her sleep, the lamp was out. 'Kerosene's over?' she muttered. From inside the hut, she could hear Ponna turning over on the cot. 'When will this girl get to sleep properly?' she said to herself.

Kali laughed. When Seerayi entered the hut to refill the kerosene lamp and to check on Ponna, he distracted her by blowing towards the portia tree and making the branch sway. And Seerayi walked out, saying, 'Hey! Are you not finished with your meddling?'

Ponna had no idea how long Kali stayed or precisely when he left.

TWELVE

Ponna slept on well past daybreak. There had been a sudden burst of rainfall at midnight. But it stopped before they could get up and move certain things indoors. Ponna had been aware of the rain. It was the kind of quick but heavy downpour that cools the heated earth. But she did not wake up, she did not see the rain, she just lay there shrivelled like a plantain leaf that had been cast aside after a feast. Vallayi was worried, seeing that even a single day's labour had taken such a toll on Ponna. They had mixed the kambu meal from last night with water. There was some curd too. The two older women waited for Ponna to wake up so that they could make her eat some of the kambu and curd. Since she did not wake up for quite a while, they both went ahead and ate a little themselves.

Outside, it did not look like it had rained at all. But they felt that it must have rained enough for one round of ploughing. The floor of the cattle shed alone was in some disarray thanks to the downpour. They cleaned that up and

94

put things back in their places. The sun grew harsh, but Ponna was still sleeping. Worried and suspicious, Vallayi went closer to check on Ponna. She was breathing steadily. It must just be the exhaustion, nothing else. Right now, the barnyard looked just like it would have if Kali had been here. The fact was that Kali was not there. That was it. Once they stepped outside and looked at the field, they could feel his absence very evidently. Everyone else's field was lush, while Kali's looked like it was a casualty to a property dispute between kinsmen and had been left uncared for. Had he been alive, he would have planted things in the two irrigated square measures of land. He had been thinking of planting chilli pepper this year. Even when he planted them in only one section of the land, he had always made sure they grew lush and healthy. They would have enough to keep harvesting for five or six months.

He would definitely have planted one square measure of ragi millets. In the rest of the land, he'd grow groundnuts and thuvarai lentils, and in the space between them he'd sow castor seeds. And bordering the groundnuts, he'd do a neat line of green grams. He would also grow kambu millets in a large plot, and maize in all the surrounding plots. This would give enough ragi and kambu to last the family over a year. There would be enough fodder for the cattle too. He'd keep the ragi stalks to feed the calves, and give the maize stalks to the bullocks. There was always fresh green grass for the milch cows. The fields were strewn with bitter orange and thumbai shrubs. The cows grazed around them. If it continued to rain, they could even sow maize.

Seerayi wondered if things would change for these fields only after the period of mourning was over and they had settled the matter of where and how Ponna was to live. Thinking along these lines, Seerayi resolved to take the cows to graze and to fetch some grass. Before setting out, she said to Vallayi, 'How long can the two of us sit around looking at each other's faces? If I go and get a bundle of grass, we can feed the milk cow. This is planting season. It is unbecoming for a farming woman like me to sit around doing nothing.'

Vallayi engaged herself in washing the pots and pans. Then she fed the hens. She sat in the front yard and observed the commotion of the blackbirds. They had started building their nest. 'Even if the older ones die, there are always new lives coming about,' she thought. She sat watching this for a little while from the flat rock bench. Then she heard the nine o'clock work siren from Karattur. She really wanted to wake Ponna up. How could a peasant woman sleep so late?

A peasant woman had to wake up at the first rooster's crow and go about making food for the day: pounding kambu and ragi grains. Then she needed to churn buttermilk. By then, the day would have started dawning. She would then pour the watery leftovers for the men to eat. After that she would have to sweep and clean the front yard and the floor of the cattle shed. If the man was a good worker and was industrious, he would milk the cow. Otherwise, the woman would have to do that too. Some of the calves would be difficult to control: they'd leap and bound about, refusing to be tied down. There are men who don't help even in such situations. If it happened to be the planting season, there was a lot more work to do. They would have to pack food and get to the fields before daybreak. Was there ever a single day when they did not have to toil? Their daily work lasted till well after it grew dark in the evening. After that, they might sleep well for the first part of the night. Then they'd be awake again.

Vallayi felt that she had been unproductive these past two months. Back home, her daughter-in-law was now doing all the work by herself. 'Well, let her also realize how useful it is to have another person's help at times like these,' Vallayi thought. It was planting season, so the farm labourers would come by to work in the fields. All the daughter-in-law had to do was take care of the domestic chores. Vallayi had come over here to make sure Ponna was not alone, but she had ended up staying on for quite a while now.

Vallayi felt that all they did was cook, eat and just hang around doing not much else. Taking the cows out for grazing and then bringing them back later—that was not much work, was it? She thought she heard Ponna muttering in her sleep. Did she have a fever? Vallayi could try touching her daughter to check for signs of fever, but she didn't want to wake her up in the bargain. Nonetheless, she stepped inside the hut to assess the situation closely.

Ponna's eyes were open. Like the eyes of a puppy that was opening its eyes to the world for the very first time, Ponna's eyelashes were crusted and stuck together. 'Amma,' she said, feebly.

Vallayi had not heard her say that in a long time. She rushed to Ponna's side lovingly and said, 'Ponna . . . what happened? Are you unwell? Do you have fever? You worked so hard yesterday, dear . . .' She placed her hand on Ponna's forehead, neck and arms to check for fever. But Ponna was fine.

'Amma, please help me up,' said Ponna. Vallayi lifted her up from the bed like she would a child. Ponna held her head in her hands and said, 'I feel dizzy.'

'You will feel fine after you eat a little. You are dehydrated. I will bring you something. You can drink it sitting right here on the cot, all right?' said Vallayi.

But Ponna said incoherently, 'No, I need to rinse my mouth first.'

'All right, walk holding on to me. You can rinse your mouth first and then drink something.' Vallayi helped Ponna walk slowly away from the cot.

Ponna found it hard to take even a single step. It felt like her feet weren't pressing down on the ground at all. It was as if her mother's shoulders were pulling her ahead. Ponna felt like laying her head down somewhere and leaning over something. She leant on her mother's shoulder. Vallayi held her by the hand and helped her walk outside. Ponna couldn't bear the harshness of the sun as soon as they stepped out. Her eyes were blinded for a few moments by the glare. She then turned to look at the portia tree. From here, she could see the entire expanse of the tree. Her mother made her sit down on the flat stone and went to fetch some water. But Ponna could not sit unsupported even for those few seconds, so she lay down on the stone. She was comforted by the warmth of the sun on her skin. She was unclear about what had happened the night before. It felt at once like a dream and a real occurrence. She ran her fingers across her chest. She could feel the scabs where the bristles on the brinjal stalks had grazed her skin. Her chest was swollen with the blood clots from these wounds. It was all his work. He wouldn't leave her alone. Not until she too joined him. 'If that's what it takes to be with you, take me with you soon,' she thought.

Her mother helped her sit up on the stone and gave her the little pitcher of water. The water was warm. It must have warmed in the sun. Ponna lacked the strength even to hold the pitcher. Her mother held it in her hands and brought it to her lips. Ponna used all the water in the pitcher to rinse her mouth thoroughly. When a little water wet her throat, she felt an intense urge to throw up. She retched so forcefully that she thought she might vomit out her innards. Holding on to the end of her mother's sari, she bent down and tried to throw up. Her mouth had pouted like the open beak of a little sparrow, but no matter how much she retched, she did not throw up. After much effort, just some saliva dribbled out. Her mother asked her to drink a little more water. But Ponna could not even close her mouth. She shook her head. Then she panted loudly. Since her mother insisted, Ponna sipped some water, but she could not take in even a mouthful. What little she drank she spat right out on her mother. She retched again as if she had a lot to vomit out. Soon she grew tired. Still keeping her mouth open and ready in case she needed to vomit, she embraced her mother in exhaustion.

Vallayi lamented, 'I don't know what has happened to you. You were well yesterday. What will I do now? Your mother-in-law is not around to help in this time of need.' As she looked about, she spotted the top of a bundle of grass over the fence by the alley. She called out, 'Seerayi, come, quick! Look at Ponna. I don't know why she is like this.' Seerayi dropped the bundle right there and came running. She thought that Ponna had done something terrible to herself. So she came beating her chest and crying out loud, 'Ayyo! You too have abandoned me and gone?' People in the adjacent fields must have heard her. But once she entered the barnyard, Seerayi saw Ponna trying hard to vomit.

She understood the situation right away. It was most definitely that. 'Ponna!' she gushed happily. 'You have given me hope. I was worried that you were going to be alone. But god has given you a new life in your womb. My son has made sure he gave us a life before he took one away from us.'

She came closer, placed her hand on Ponna's head and then cracked her knuckles to ward off the evil eye. Ponna could not make sense of anything yet. But now Vallayi too understood the situation. To confirm it, she asked, 'Ponna, how long has it been since your last period?' But Ponna had not really kept track of it. She did not recollect it happening since Kali's death. Vallayi said, 'That god has not forsaken us. Your own husband has now come as a child in your womb. There is nothing to worry about now.'

Ponna understood at last. But she held her head in her hands and burst into sobs.

THIRTEEN

All those in the adjacent fields who had heard Seerayi's loud laments now landed up at the barnyard. It was quite a large crowd. But once they found out what the situation really was, all the men dispersed, saying, 'These womenfolk are always like this. They would yell when good things happen, yell when bad things happen. I dropped everything and ran over here because I thought there has been another death.'

None of the women left. They went over to Ponna and wished her well. When she looked up at each of their faces, all she could do was weep. The women stood around talking among themselves, feeling a mixture of both happiness and sadness.

'What an unlucky fellow. Such bad timing, his death. He was not fortunate enough to look at her now.'

'This is his doing. He has given a life in exchange for taking one. It is going to be a boy, you wait and see.'

'It must be the third month now, that's why she experiences this kind of retching.'

'Actually, she might have experienced this sooner had they added seasoning to their food. They were not doing that because they are still in the mourning period. If she had smelt the hot crackling of seasoning in the oil, she'd have retched a while ago.'

'No one noticed that her menses was delayed?'

'Right! When they are grieving the loss of the man of the house, who has the time to notice when menses is supposed to happen!'

'Apparently, all the astrologers they consulted told them they would definitely have a child. Instead of being patient, he went ahead and hung himself just because some useless dog insulted him. Such pride.'

Everyone had something to say about this new development.

Ponna sat there, crying and retching.

'Ponna . . . why are you crying? Now your future looks hopeful. When you have a child running around you, life becomes a little easier. Don't worry,' said Thorattu Paatti from Nonikkaadu, lifting Ponna's face by her hand. That old woman had no children of her own. Her husband died when she was very young. She moved here to live in her brother's home and had spent all her life here. Now this paatti too felt like crying when she looked at Ponna. She sang:

Even when you are draped in silk
when four palanquins wait on you

when you have gold to wear
even when you live well and well
if you don't have a child
what's the point, where's the pride?
Where's the joy of kith and kin?
Now a child has come
Ponna, your life
now has a point, now has its pride
it also has the joy of kith and kin.

Everybody laughed and rejoiced at paatti's singing. Some made fun of her: 'If you don't stop her, she might gather people and start kummi dancing right here, right now!' Wiping away Ponna's tears with her fingers, Thorattu Paatti said, 'I am the kind of person who prays that no one should have to endure the struggles I went through. I was quite sad thinking of you. Even when we have our siblings and relatives, there is nothing like having someone who is entirely ours, is there?'

A cheeky young fellow said, addressing Thorattu Paatti, but hiding his face in the crowd, 'Paatti, I will go and say this to your brother's grandson. Let me see what happens then.'

Thorattu Paatti replied, 'Sure, go tell him gladly. Only I know what my struggles have been. What does he know?' But seeing that Ponna could still not stop retching, Thorattu Paatti turned to Seerayi and said, 'Pound a peppercorn and a little dried ginger into a powder, add some karuppatti, and make her drink the extract. All this retching will stop. Then prepare something for her to eat, something she is really fond of. This child is a belated arrival. Take very good care of her.' Only after Thorattu Paatti spoke to her did Seerayi collect herself and find her bearings. She lit the fire in the stove with a few twigs. Vallayi felt a little embarrassed that she had not been quick to figure out why Ponna was feeling unwell.

Seerayi set a potful of water on the stove. She felt happy that so many people had gathered on hearing the good news. It would have been so much better if Kali had been here to celebrate this moment. But she was filled with so much joy that she did not dwell on that. 'I came running, thinking something terrible has happened. I had just reached near the well when I heard her mother shouting to me. What was I to think! I completely panicked; Ponna has been languishing in his memory, what if she has done something to herself? Anybody would panic in such a situation. It is only natural, right? That's why I yelled. I threw away the grass bundle right there and came rushing here, and that's when I saw that she was feeling nauseated. That's when I remembered that she had not had her menses since his death. I am delighted that god has given us some hope,' said Seerayi as she opened the spice box. She found pepper there, but no dried ginger.

She said to Vallayi, 'I had bought some dried ginger sometime ago. I think it is back home in the village. Valla, sister, please wash her face with some water and make her lie down on the cot. I will quickly run and get the dried ginger,' and she trotted out of the barnyard.

Some people who saw her running down the alley remarked, 'Look at Seerayi's delight. She will become very busy from now on.' Seerayi's heart was definitely buoyant with joy. 'Ponna is pregnant,' she shared the news with them. But she did not say anything more to anyone. When she reached the village, some people asked her, 'Seerayikka, is it true that your daughter-in-law is pregnant?' She said, 'Has the news already reached this far? Yes, it is true. We just found out today,' and kept on walking. One woman asked, 'How many months has it been? Seven or eight?' Seerayi did not even stop to look at the woman's face. She said, 'Which cunning woman is that? If this was the seventh or the eighth month, wouldn't we have known already? If that was the case, why would my son die such a gruesome death? This is like asking for cooking fuel from a house that is burning down. It was our bad time. God has chosen to show us some kindness only after Kali is no more. Think well of us.' She kept running as she said this, and when she reached her house, she ran in, opened the spice box and picked out some dried ginger.

'If anyone says anything cheeky, I will burn that tongue the way I am going to roast this piece of dried ginger. But then, this is our time of misfortune. It is only natural that those who are doing well will say whatever comes to their mind. We lose nothing by letting it all play out. All we need is for our bad time to run itself out,' she said to herself. On her way back, she spoke a little to everyone she encountered on her path.

As she was passing the village's common well, she came across Kaaraan standing there with a pot in his hand. When he saw her, he said, 'Aaya, can you draw a pot of water for me, please?'

She said, 'Of course,' and obliged him. Then she said to him, 'Kaaraan, my daughter-in-law, Ponna, is pregnant. We need to convey this to the in-laws in Adaiyur. Can you go?'

Kaaraan said, 'You mean our landlady Ponna? Of course I can go. Let me drop off this pot of water at home first. Then I will go right away.'

'Ponna's family will be so happy that they are sure to reward you for bringing the news. You might even get a new dhoti. They will start and come over right away as soon as you give them the news. But you also formally invite them.'

'Definitely,' he said. 'I will tell them to get the cart ready and head over here right away. It is just sad that Kali was not lucky enough to hear this news . . .'

That remark trailed in the air as Seerayi had already taken off towards the barnyard. She suddenly realized that she had forgotten to inform the midwife. The midwife lived at the other end of the village. If Seerayi went there now, she'd be delayed. So she decided to find someone else to fetch the midwife. As she walked on the path that led from the village out to the fields, she saw a woman walking towards her, her face concealed by the bundle of grass she was carrying on her head. Seerayi could not recognize her by her gait. But as the person came closer, she saw that it was Pongayi from Mosakkaadu.

She was a good woman; she never wished ill of others. She had taken good care of a husband who died drinking. Then she raised two daughters and a son all by herself. Pongayi had visited them in the barnyard just a few days ago, and she had cried, saying, 'How terrible that things have happened this way. Is this all there is to human life?'

Seerayi stopped her and gave her the news. 'Ponga, can you go tell the midwife to come right away, please?'

Ponga said, 'You go and make the dried ginger potion for Ponna. I will go tell the midwife, it is only a little out of my way. Even if the man is not at home, the midwife will certainly be. She will come right away. You know Ponna is pregnant, but you will feel much better if the midwife herself says it. I will tell her, don't worry.'

Seerayi walked on with a new strength in her heart, and a gentle breeze brushed past her like the touch of a flower.

FOURTEEN

Ponna lay down on the cot. Now she felt absolutely certain. Kali had definitely paid her a visit the night before. He had spent a lot of time with her. And *he* had placed this new life within her. As long as he had been alive, he could not accomplish that. But now he had. He had given up his life just so he could solve Ponna's problem. He had done that just for her good. She could now recollect all the words he had spoken to her before sending her into a sleepy haze. Even now, she could hear his voice, and it made her dizzy. 'I am here to give you what you want.' And he had. What day was it yesterday? Thursday. Kali had died on a Thursday. It was exactly two months since he died. The beginning of the third month.

He was not angry with her. He wanted to only help her out. She thought again about the night before. She could recollect the feeling of being immersed in great pleasure, the kind of pleasure she had not experienced ever before. She could recall that feeling even now. This retching was the result of that. Kali was like an expert magician who could manipulate what people could see. 'Maama,' she moaned. 'All right, you are within me now. I am not going to let go of you. But please don't be born as a male child. Your grandfather did not live long. Nor did your father. Nor you. Give me a girl child. I will raise her well and make your name proud. She will lie on my lap just like you used to. I will give her these breasts to feed from. Let the family's curse end with you. If it is a male child, then a girl like me would have to marry him and struggle just the way I am struggling now. I don't want that. You promised to give me what I want. *This* is what I want.' Ponna was muttering all this in her dizziness.

Most of the women who had come to the barnyard to see Ponna had left by then, after remarking that all would now be well for Ponna. Only a few elderly women who had come to gather some greens from the fields now lingered about. Seeing Seerayi rushing back into the barnyard, one of them asked, 'Were you able to find some dried ginger, Seerayi?'

'Yes, aaya, I always keep these things in the spice box. After all, if we need something like this urgently, where can we go looking? It is good to have some handy,' said Seerayi as she pounded and powdered a piece of dried ginger and dropped it into some boiling water. She took out some karuppatti that she was carrying in a fold in her sari, broke it down with the head of a churner, and added that to the water as well. The fire had gone out. So she put in a dried palmyra and blew towards the stove to rekindle the fire.

Looking at Vallayi, she asked, 'So, what is your daughter saying?'

'My daughter?' replied Vallayi. 'She is your daughter-in-law. You pamper her. She is lying in a daze. I am worried about how she is going to find her bearings and come out of this state.'

Seerayi said, 'You are the mother. Stay by her, feed her tasty and tangy meat, and help her regain strength.' She filtered out the ginger extract after smelling the fragrance to make sure it was ready. Then she poured it back and forth between the pot and its lid to cool it down. Handing it over to Vallayi, she said, 'Go, give this to her. I have not made it into a potion. More like dried-ginger tea. And it is just the right temperature. It will be good for the throat. I will use the same fire and put some rice to boil. That's what she would like to eat now. We can make some watery lentils without any seasoning. She will be able to drink that.'

Vallayi helped Ponna sit up and managed to have her drink the ginger extract sip by sip. After just two sips, Ponna burped loudly.

Thena Paatti, who was sitting outside, said, 'Yes, it will make you burp. Drink slowly, in small sips.' She then addressed Seerayi, 'Hey, Seera, the period of mourning is not over yet, is it? Then how can you cook rice?'

Seerayi had been expecting this question, so she was ready with the reply: 'This is the farmstead, isn't it, aaya? We are not supposed to cook rice inside the house. It should be all right to do so here in the barnyard. For two months now, we have just been camping here like nomads, cooking and eating right here. We haven't even lit the stove back home. On the day the period of blockage is over and we go to the hill temple, we can clean the house properly and do everything ritually right. But for now, I can cook for her here. Look at her suffering. She will feel better only if she can eat something she likes. All these observances are things we decide, aren't they? What do you feel? Do you agree, Thorattu Paatti?' She roped in the other woman for support.

'Yes,' the woman agreed. 'What's the big deal? Cooking rice here now is just the same as cooking it in someone else's house and bringing it here. Go ahead and make her some rice, Seerayi. If Kali objects to it, let him come and say so.'

The elderly women were all sitting in the shade of the portia tree. Thorattu Paatti took out her waist pouch. Looking at the pouch, Thena Paatti made fun of her. 'You never let that bag get too far from your waist. Looks like you have told everyone they can touch that pouch only after you are dead, and use the money for your final rites! It seems to have quite a lot in it. See how swollen it is!'

Thorattu Paatti rejoindered, 'All I have in it is some betel leaves and tobacco. And some lime paste. You can take a look if you want,' and she pulled out the pouch's contents. All of them partook of the betel leaves.

Seerayi was listening to their banter while she cooked. Ponna drank very little of the lentil-rice meal Seerayi made for her, but she felt better after that minor replenishment. By then, Thangayi, the midwife, walked in, remarking, 'All of you elders are gathered here. I wondered if someone has died.'

Thorattu Paatti retorted, 'Well, you will certainly be glad if something big and bad had happened, won't you?'

And Thangayi replied, 'Yes. The four of you must be over eighty years old. I am waiting for at least one of you to drop dead, so that I can enjoy some feasts for a few days. But it does not seem to happen.'

One of the elders said, 'Your husband makes money shaving people. Isn't that enough for you? You want to live off people dying too?'

Thangayi carried on as if she did not hear that remark at all: 'Hale and healthy people like our Kali end up dying young. But nothing seems to happen to the old and worn-out ones. Sure, go ahead and live on till you are a hundred.'

'Why don't you give us some poison and kill us? We will be happy to go,' said Thorattu Paatti.

They all knew that Thangayi always teased people this way. She never said anything that really upset anyone. She was the midwife for the entire village. She treated all the women, and she also took care of the deliveries. Even though her husband's main job was as a barber, he also worked as a medic for the men. They got a total annual payment for all their services. Thangayi now lifted Ponna's right hand and felt her pulse. 'Kali's life has now blossomed inside her. It is confirmed. Tomorrow morning, I will give her four balls of herbal medicine. She should eat it once a day for four days. All this retching will stop,' she said. Ponna smiled at her weakly. Thangayi continued, adding her good wishes, 'There is a smile on her face. Everything will go well; she will deliver a good, healthy child. This family will flourish and grow stronger; a little one will play around here and prosper.' Vallayi brought one measure, about eight cups, of kambu millets and poured it into the waist fold of Thangayi's sari. The midwife secured it carefully and then stepped outside the hut.

Thorattu Paatti now said to her, 'You talk too much these days. We should ask your husband to cut off your tongue a little.'

'That is not going to happen,' another woman interjected. 'He worships her.'

'Oh, is that so? How does he pray? On his knees or fully lying down?'

'He does it standing up,' Thangayi replied. 'Look at the things these old ones say!'

'Be careful, woman. The man walks around with a knife in his hand.'

'But Thangayi has the stone on which he can sharpen his knife,' said another bawdily.

All these elderly women, these paattis, were having a lot of fun and laughter with this banter.

Thangayi then said to Thorattu Paatti, 'Can I have some betel leaves?' The old woman pulled out her waist pouch again. 'This old woman is so reluctant to open that pouch!'

But Thorattu Paatti didn't let that remark go. She said, 'Right. All I have is this waist purse. You clearly have a golden pouch, which you are quick to open and share,' and gave Thangayi half a betel leaf and a nut.

'Why can't you give me a full leaf? What will you lose? How is this enough?'

And Thorattu Paatti said, 'Our betel leaves cannot satisfy a mouth, can they?'

'I can never win talking to you,' said Thangayi. 'Give me some lime. I will get going. I have a lot of work to do.'

Another paatti said, 'Take that betel leaf safely back home and ask your husband for some white-lime paste.'

'Yes, yes, I know. I am so glad to see all of you sitting here, chatting happily. May this happiness last,' she wished wholeheartedly.

When Thorattu Paatti said 'Happy, happy midwife' in a sing-song tone, all the other women joined in and clapped their hands in the kummi fashion.

Happy, happy midwife,
is that the sound of ankle bells, oh midwife?
We hear the jiggling of kambu millets, oh midwife,
do add some jaggery to it, oh midwife,
make sure you close the door, oh midwife
crush it carefully, oh midwife.

Thangayi ran away, saying, 'These old women won't stop teasing me today. I am off!' Someone lewdly commented,

'Hey! Be careful, hold on to the kambu properly'—she was punning on the other meaning of 'kambu'—a pole. But Thangayi did not even respond to that before leaving.

The scent of boiling rice wafted out. Seerayi was cooking lentils on the other stove. She now said to Vallayi, 'Sister, these paattis have grown tired with all the singing. Dilute some of the kambu millets for them. Let them drink some and take rest. It is midday already.'

One of the paattis said, 'If you have some curd, do make some buttermilk for us. There is no time now to go home for lunch. We will just drink some here, lie down for a bit under the portia tree and leave in the evening.'

Seerayi replied, 'Why not? You can also stay the night if you want to. I will lay two cots under the tree for you.'

'But your son sits on this portia tree.'

'Let him sit on the tree, that stupid fellow. You can be in the shade. Is he going to claim the shade too?'

'What can he do to us? If he takes us, we will go with him happily. Why do we need to go on living, burdening this earth?'

Before Vallayi could dilute the millets for the women, Seerayi had finished cooking the lentils and churned them properly into an easily digestible broth. She put some rice and lentils on a plate and took it to Ponna. When Ponna took the plate from Seerayi and set it down on her lap, the fragrance from the hot food rose to her nose.

For the first time in a long while, looking at that steaming plate of food, Ponna felt the desire to eat.

116

FIFTEEN

Just like Seerayi had predicted, Ponna's father and brother came over immediately in their bullock cart. They even brought along Muthu's wife and son. As if they had come bearing wedding gifts, they unloaded several small sacks from the cart. Some brass cooking vessels too. They had brought dried grains, various kinds of lentils, karuppatti, coconut and several other things.

Ponna's sister-in-law, Poovayi, rushed to her and embraced her. 'Better times ahead, finally,' she said.

All the elderly women, the paattis who had been resting in the shade of the portia tree, sat up and talked among themselves, muttering, 'Had Kali been alive, they'd have brought even more lavish gifts.'

'This is nothing. If it is a male child, the uncle would bring enormous gifts.'

'The uncle already has a boy. If this happens to be a girl child, they can marry each other. Muthu has one child, and

117

Ponna will have one. Both wealth and relations, everything will stay within the family.'

'Well, that's what we wish, but it is important that god wishes the same.'

'That's right. If all our wishes come true, then what's the point of a god?'

'You are right. He might even act contrarily just to spite us. That is why a lot of people do not ask god for specific things. They just pray to him to do as he sees fit.'

And so the women sat and talked about such things.

Meanwhile, Seerayi and Vallayi were busy recounting everything from the beginning, proudly talking about how they realized Ponna was pregnant. Ponna appeared to be a bit more energetic after eating her meal. She walked, holding her sister-in-law's hand, and emerged from the hut and sat down on the stone. Her sister-in-law undid Ponna's hair and rubbed oil on it. Ponna had not taken care of her hair for several days, so it looked like a palm sheath, all tangled up. 'Make sure you wash this oil out in time, using some herbal powder. Otherwise, it will become hard to untangle your hair fully,' she said to Ponna as she used a comb to loosen up the tangles. She did it very gently, turning Ponna's head this way and that, making sure the comb did not pull too hard and hurt Ponna. Ponna was still not fully aware of everything happening around her. She had not expected her mother and mother-in-law to be this happy at the news. Then, there was the happiness expressed by the people of the village, with everyone visiting her. And now, gifts from her natal family. Everyone looked radiant. Just one person's pregnancy brings joy to so many people.

Ponna felt that she could now begin to grasp why people considered childlessness such a great misfortune. A child contains within itself the possibility of great joy and celebration. If this was how people responded at the beginning, Ponna wondered how things would be when the child was delivered. Nangai was full of advice and suggestions: 'You will feel this retching sensation in the morning. Don't force yourself to throw up. Your throat will go sore. Just pop a small piece of karuppatti. It will help ease the retching. If you don't wake up too quickly but just lie around for a while before getting up, you will feel less dizzy. Then as the day progresses, you will feel much stronger. Don't tire yourself out, only do the chores you can do. Once you enter the fifth month, all this vomiting will stop. Then you can feel normal.'

Seerayi turned to Muthu and said, 'My dear boy, we need to look ahead now. Your friend acted in haste and is gone now. It is true that we would all have been happier if he were still here, but he is not going to return just because we spend all our time thinking of him. It looks like this child was destined to come only after taking the father away. From now on, we rely on your help. It rained last night. If Kali had been here, he'd have secured the bulls to the plough first thing in the morning. It is a little too late for kambu millets and groundnuts. But we can still scatter maize all over the field. That will also give us enough to feed the few cattle we have here. We can also feed them the grass that will grow. Let Vallayi take care of the house and the girl. I will work in the fields. You please help us.'

'We still have a good part of the day left, Atthai,' said Muthu. 'I will sow maize today in one long measure of land. We can do the rest tomorrow. I will make sure we do the sowing when the soil is still wet. We won't leave anything undone.'

'That's right, Muthu,' said Seerayi. 'When we have a life growing here in the house, the field too should be tended to. That's the right way to do things. The family will thrive just as the land does. So, yes, please do the sowing today. I don't know how much maize he has kept. There won't be enough to sow over the entire land. He would have planned to focus on kambu and groundnuts and would have kept just enough maize for the remaining land. Let us ask Ponna, she would know. Otherwise, we can just go take a look in the storage room ourselves.'

Muthu set out right away to the field to see where he could begin sowing. He still did not feel he had the courage to look Ponna in the eye. What would he say to her? It was the visit to the temple festival that had given her this child. So the problem had never been with her. It had been with Kali. What would Kali have thought about this had he been alive? Would he have felt hurt that this child had come to make it known to the world that he was the deficient one? Or would he have rejoiced that the village could taunt them no more for being childless? This child has been given by some god. But if you think about it, we are all children given by god. Also, there is no family where the lineage has been straight and pure. Every family has some story it wishes to downplay. There is no family about which someone doesn't say—she went there, he went there. Why, even his own father, when he was angry with him, would occasionally remark, 'Who knows whom you were born to?' Clearly, he harboured some such ideas himself. If one were to think about it, all those stories about people changing, or castes changing, or villages changing, or even countries changing—they all make sense somehow.

In Sevvoor, there is something called the Vellaiyan Kaadu—the White Man's Field. Muthu learnt about it when he went there to do some paid ploughing work. In that family that hired him, he noticed that at least one person of every generation was born very fair-skinned, just like a white foreigner. But they took pride in that fair skin. Even the farmer who owned that land was quite fair-complexioned. It was he who said to Muthu, 'Long ago, in our family, there was a very attractive woman. She was dark-skinned like all our people were, but apparently, she had a kind of radiance and everyone found her attractive. After her marriage, she went with her husband to watch the temple chariot. A white officer who saw her there forcefully took her with him. The husband too followed them and waited outside the white man's bungalow. Apparently, he sat there the whole night. After all, he could not have just left his wife there with the white man, could he? Nor could he fight and protest against him. The next day, she came out crying—while the white man emerged, grinning, and even patted this man on his back, implying that the man was lucky to have such an attractive wife. The white man also offered him a wad of cash. But the husband didn't take it. He wept. The white man wondered what gift would make him happy and then decided to give him ten acres of unclaimed common land. If you offer land to a farmer, he'd forget everything else, he'd give you anything. That's how this land came to us, you see. Thanks to that foremother of ours. There was no way we could have got land like this by ourselves. The seed that the white man sowed still keeps coming down the generations. In each generation a boy or girl is born white-skinned. And this name, White Man's Field, has stuck. In this village, people do marry outside their caste, but it all happens hush-hush. But everyone knew about that woman in our family going with the white man. So I am frank about it. When people come to marry into our family, we let them know that the child is likely to be born fair-skinned.' He also added, 'When a child is born fair, no one seems to mind. They take pride in it.' So everything boils down to our perspective on things.

Muthu looked at the field. All the squares of land seemed to be in good shape, their raised boundaries all in proper condition. He chose a square of land in which the soil was still moist, and started plucking away the kolunji plants that had been growing there. It occurred to Muthu that this land too has been touched and handled by various people. Once a person takes it over from the earlier owner, they carry on with the ploughing and sowing, don't they? Muthu said to himself that he needed to do all he could to make sure Ponna didn't suffer. There was nothing he could do about the void created by Kali's death. The couple had been very happy together. Kali had given up everything for Ponna and had stayed confined to this barnyard. But before Kali and Ponna had got married, Muthu and Kali had gone looking for women at least once a month. So later when Kali asked for Ponna's hand in marriage, even though Muthu happily agreed to it on the outside, he was anxious in his heart, wondering if Kali would mend his ways or not. Muthu had not at all expected how faithful Kali had stayed to Ponna. She had kept him under her control—if he was so much as friendly with the sort of person she disapproved of, she inevitably made her displeasure known.

Kali had said to Muthu several times in the past, 'The best thing you have done for me is to have given your sister in marriage to me.' Muthu now felt that if Kali had stopped to think about their friendship, he wouldn't have ended his life. Kali had come to think of Ponna as his own precious property. Muthu felt very lonely there without Kali. When he had plucked away half a field of kolunji plants, he heard his father call out to him, 'Hey, boy!' After Kali's death, Muthu's father had started being more affectionate towards him. Even though he yelled back, 'I am coming, I am coming,' he left only after he finished weeding out all the kolunji growth and tying it in a bundle. The kolunji shoots were still fresh, some still had flowers on them. If he dumped them all into a pit, they'd make good manure. Kali had always thought of such small ideas and details. Muthu walked on, feeling that even though Kali himself had gone, he had left his thoughts and ideas behind. But Muthu could not help wondering how different things would have been if Kali himself had still been with them.

SIXTEEN

Muthu did not know anything at all about that particular custom. But his father seemed to be aware of it. It was good that Thorattu Paatti reminded them.

At dusk, when the sun grew less harsh, all the paattis got ready to leave. From the gifts that had come from Ponna's village, they were given two bananas and a piece of karuppatti each, which they bundled up in the folds of their saris. Kulla Paatti said, 'You are giving so much even to us old women. What did you give Kaaraan who brought you the good news?'

Muthu replied, 'We rewarded him to his heart's content, aaya.'

After hearing the news from Seerayi, Kaaraan had set out immediately to convey it to Ponna's family. Anyone in his place would have agreed to do the task. Any young boy would have loved to run and convey the news and pocket the reward. That was why Kaaraan did not tell anyone else the news. He had cut across the fields, taking shortcuts to carry out his errand. On the way, he had met Muthu in the fields and given him the message. In his excitement, Muthu had embraced and lifted Kaaraan up and said, 'What wonderful news you have brought us!' The man was embarrassed. 'Saami! Please let go of me before anyone sees us.' Muthu said, 'All right. Come over to the house,' and ran, leaping in joy. By the time Kaaraan reached their house, Muthu had already kept a dhoti, a towel and two rupees for Kaaraan. Offering these to him, Muthu had said, 'Is this enough?' Kaaraan had been beside himself with joy. He then had his lunch with them there and left with them in their cart. Before Kaaraan had parted ways with them, Muthu had asked him to find a woman labourer to help Ponna and Seerayi with the work in their field.

Thena Paatti asked for some betel leaf and nut, and chewing a mouthful of them, she said, 'Everything will go well. Ponna will have a good delivery and she will raise the child well. Anyway, we are all here to help. Please send for us if you need anything. We will come and cook delicious meals for her. If the same person does all the cooking all the time, it becomes monotonous. There will be some variety if different people make even the same dish.'

'Make sure you inform the village council of this news,' Thorattu Paatti said. 'Even I forgot about it.'

That was when Muthu heard about the custom. If a woman is pregnant when her husband is dead, the village council had to be informed. There would be an elaborate ceremony, beginning on the day of the dead husband's final rites, when the entire village would gather. Once the funeral procession returned home from the cremation grounds and finished the prayers at home, a barber would stand at the entrance to the house and set down a pitcher full of water next to him. The wife would come to that spot still clad in the wet sari in which she had her bath and touch and pay respects to the pot of water. Then the barber would speak loudly: 'I have some news to share in this gathering of close kinsmen, uncles, brothers-in-law, other people of the caste, and of the village. The thing is that this woman who married on such-and-such a date and now stands clad in white, her husband—who was so-and-so's son, who is from such-and-such a place, from such-and-such a field— departed for the other world on such-and-such a time on such-and-such a day, my lords. On this day, when we are offering our prayer so that he should not face any obstacles on his path to god, his chaste wife stands here to inform the village that he has left behind a foetus in her womb. They calculate that it has been so many months and so many days and the foetus is so-much old. They might be ten or twenty days off the mark, but those are god's calculations. Since she is going through the unbearable sadness of the loss of her husband, I, as a member of this community, standing in front of this council, am informing everyone of it on her behalf, my lords. All of you should receive this news without making any untoward comments, my lords.'

He would deliver that speech loudly so that everybody could hear. Then, an elder from the village would respond on behalf of everyone else: 'All right. We accept this information. Now carry on and do what needs to be done.' Then, a married woman would walk towards the widow—who, till that moment, would be standing there, hands folded and head bowed—and lead her into the house.

The rationale behind this custom was to prevent anyone from saying later that she managed to get pregnant after her husband's death. If they did not know until after the final rites that the wife was pregnant, the custom was to still inform the village council. They would have to ask the village headman to call for a meeting, and a person from the family had to go and stand in front of the gathering and make the news known. Otherwise, the council would excommunicate the family. Only after the paatti reminded them about this did all of them realize that the custom needed to be carried out. They had forgotten because it had been quite a long time since such a situation had come about. After they consulted the village headman and decided on a date for the meeting, they had to send someone to inform everyone about it. At the meeting, when the news is shared, close kinsmen have to be present. Kali was an only child. So was his father and even his grandfather. So there was really no one within the village who could be called his immediate kinsman.

But there were families in the village who could be considered close kin. According to custom, Seerayi had to personally go and inform all these close relatives and also the entire village. So Muthu said to her, 'Atthai, you first go and speak to the village headman. Take my father with you. Once we know when the village council meeting will be, we can go in the morning to all the close relatives and invite them personally. You will have to go. I don't mind going, but if I do, they will ask how a brother-in-law could be sent to do that.'

Seerayi thus set out with Muthu's father to meet the village leader. Thorattu Paatti said, as she walked out with them, 'The purpose is to let the village know that this foetus was conceived when the husband was still alive. That the wife did not get this by going to some random man.'

Ponna overheard that remark. After her sister-in-law finished combing her hair, Ponna went to the cot and lay curled up. All the affection she had felt for Kali earlier that day had now dried up. Kali had put her in a demeaning situation where she had to stand in front of the entire village and declare: 'I slept only with my husband.' What would the village do if she were to say, 'This child is not his. I slept with a stranger'? Kali had visited her the night before and spoken sweet words of love. What would he do tonight? Would he come to her rescue, seeing how she had to stand and defend herself in front of the villagers? Ponna felt that Kali would perhaps continuously torment her even in his death. She did not know how to let go of him.

Ponna lay face down on the cot, crying. Vallayi came to her, touched her gently on the head and consoled her, 'Don't lie on your stomach, my dear. You should only lie on your side from now on. Don't cry. It is our fate that we

129

have to endure all this. Think of it as fate. He is gone, but we have to live on. And we can't do that if we antagonize the entire village, can we? All you need to do is go and stand there.'

Ponna got up and turned to lie on her side. Poovayi, her sister-in-law, said to Vallayi, 'I will be with her. You go.' She then said to Ponna, after the old woman had left, 'Why are you crying? You should not cry when you are with child. All of us are standing by you. Why do you have to worry then? The village has certain customs. What do they know of how much these things hurt us women? If he knew of the humiliation you would have to endure going and standing there in front of everyone, would he have killed himself? But then, it is not as if men who are alive and well understand women's miseries either. Don't think too much about these things. If the custom demands it, just get it done. How many temples you have visited, how many prayers you have offered—thousands of them. And all of those have borne fruit now. Remember that and hold on to that happiness in your heart. If this didn't happen, you would have had to be all alone. A brother or a father can support you only so far. But you now have someone to call your own. Think about that and be happy. If we take on everything as a struggle, it would be nothing but struggles all the way.'

Ponna wondered if it was time to move back to the house in the village. She felt she should not stay any longer at the barnyard. Her earlier reason for staying there was that it would help her live close to the memories of Kali.

But if she continued to stay on, he would continue to make life difficult for her. She even wondered whether she should move to her mother's house until the delivery.

She was angry with Kali.

SEVENTEEN

The village council meeting was scheduled for the Friday of
the following week. It always took place on Fridays unless
some emergency meeting had to be called for. By then,
news about the meeting had reached everyone. Within
the main part of the village, there were only ten or fifteen
households. So they had to dispatch the man who made
announcements in the village to go and inform those who
lived spread out among the fields. Seerayi went in person
to inform the washerman and the barber. The washerman
had only the job of laying out the cloth for the ritual. It
was the barber who had a key role to play. Muthu gave
him five rupees and told him to buy all that was needed for
the meeting. When Seerayi tried to object to him paying,
Muthu said she needn't worry and that he'd take care
of things.

There were seventeen houses as far as close kinsmen
were concerned. Seerayi went to all of them in person
to invite them to the meeting. 'I don't know why that

132

goddess Kooli is so angry with our family,' she said to them carefully. 'She is piling so much misery upon us. I was worried that she was pushing us all into the grave, but now she seems to have sent down a little creeper for us to hold on to and climb out. We need to hold on to it carefully without breaking it, and climb out of our graves. It seems I have swallowed my husband as well as my son; I am a lonely widow. The only ray of hope and strength I now have is that my daughter-in-law is pregnant. In this village, who else do I have to call my own, but you. I don't have any other close kinsmen. You have to be present at all our occasions.'

Muthu had performed the final rites for Kali. And this had produced some discontent among these relatives. So they asked her, with taunting smiles, 'You didn't think of us during the final rites, Seerayi. But somehow we came to your mind only now?'

Seerayi had expected this question to surface sooner or later. 'That issue would not have arisen if we had only one family we could consider as close kin,' she calmly explained. 'There are so many of you. And I didn't know which of you to call. If I reach out to one of you, the others take offence. Moreover, on the day, I could not think clearly about anything. I was suffering, thinking about how so many men in our families seem to die, leaving their womenfolk to struggle alone. In the middle of all that despair, when the question came up as to who would perform the final rites, his brother-in-law came forward right away. He loved Kali very much. They had been friends since childhood. In fact, that was why they even gave their daughter in marriage to Kali. So when he stepped forward to do the rites, I could not object. I decided to let him do it since I thought it might also console him. If he had died after living a long life, I'd have called all of your womenfolk and asked them to prepare various food items according to tradition, and offer them to the crows. And I'd have given them all gifts. He took his life, leaving two women to fend for themselves. What is the point in splitting hairs about rituals for him? And just for the sake of custom, his brother-in-law's wife placed the food on the roof for the crows to eat. Oh, my dear boy, my god, is this fair? We kept the food for the crows on the roof, and waited and waited, and no crow came, no crow cawed, it was not your time to go, Kaliyappa! Kaliyappa! Your accounts are not settled. Your time hadn't come, your time hadn't come!'

She ended with a dirge. And the women among these relatives consoled her, saying, 'Seerayi akka, please don't cry. We shouldn't have raised that now. Only women understand other women's struggles. How can we not show up for you? We will send our men. And we will be there too.'

Seerayi also went to her natal family to invite them to the meeting. She had two younger brothers. She had been on good terms with them once. As a little boy, Kali would go to spend time at his uncles' homes. But the uncles were upset that Kali did not let them find a girl for him to marry and instead found one himself. So they stopped visiting, and their relationship with Kali had soured. Had he married someone related to them, or suggested by them, then there would have been a brisk exchange of marital gifts and a lot of coming and going and strengthening of bonds. And since he did not have a child of his own, they had started coveting his wealth and had been speaking suggestively about it. Several years ago, they had also invited him to the village temple festival in their parts. Kali and Ponna had both planned to go to the festival, but Ponna ended up having a major tussle with the older uncle's wife—and the family took umbrage at this.

This had happened in the seventh year of their marriage. Both uncles' families had come in person and invited them to the village temple festival. The older uncle's wife had told them very affectionately that Kali and Ponna should go early and be there in the morning of the day they would make pongal for the goddess. Seerayi too had insisted that they should go since they had been invited personally. Kali had asked Ponna to go before him, and said that he would join her once he had seen to the cows and calves. So Ponna had set out, carrying two bunches of bananas. Thalaiyur was not too far away, just five miles. She had eaten some gruel and left soon after dawn, and she reached her destination by the time the sun was in her line of sight. No other relatives had arrived by then. They were all to arrive later in the day.

Ponna had a lot of work to do as soon as she got there. She had to pound the flour for the lamp ritual and grind batter for vadai, in addition to several other tasks. She had got started as soon as she arrived. The older uncle's wife had taken both bunches of bananas that Ponna had brought, and put them away. Ponna had intended one of the banana bunches for the other uncle's household, but she did not say anything right away. She had decided she would bring that up later while leaving from there. In the afternoon, they had been boiling and reducing jaggery and rolling flour balls. There had been a large quantity of kambu flour, enough rice flour for the lamp, and just enough chickpea flour to make four or five balls. Apparently, the older uncle's son really liked the sweet balls made with the chickpea flour. So even though it was expensive, they had included at least a small quantity.

As they sat rolling these balls, the aunt had chatted with Ponna. She asked, 'You are on good terms with your older brother, aren't you?'

'Yes, yes,' Ponna had replied. 'Definitely. In fact, my brother and husband are close friends. They don't even bother that much when I don't visit, but if he doesn't go, someone comes over personally to fetch him.'

'Yes, that's what the entire village is saying. But be careful. Don't write off your wealth to your brother just because you don't have children.'

Ponna did not like the direction the conversation was taking. 'We are still young,' she had ventured. 'We don't have to worry about all that now.'

'No, Ponna. You don't know about these things. My husband and his younger brother are very fond of their sister, Seerayi, and they shower her with a lot of gifts. If we, the wives, object, they shut us up, saying that she is a widow and only has her brothers to care for her. So basically, all our wealth has gone there, you see.'

Ponna could not contain her anger at this. She had slammed down the mass of flour she had been kneading back in the bowl. 'What gifts have you really showered on my mother-in-law? It was only after my marriage that some four copper cauldrons and brass carriers entered that house, and that's because I brought them. Before that all they had was a mud pot and another one with its mouth broken. And what happened to the gifts you say the brothers lavished on their sister? Does she have walls gilded with gold? You are coveting our wealth now when we are still young and healthy. I won't be surprised if you kill us and take our things. Now I understand why you have been so unctuous and friendly. Earn and save for your son and daughter. Don't eye heirless property elsewhere and dangle your tongue in greed!' With that, she had left right away and returned home. Then she did not let Kali go to the festival either.

For Seerayi, these people were the only other family she had. Her own brothers. She had already warned Ponna, 'Don't come back telling me the things they said to you about me. They are my brothers' families. They will say unpleasant things. Just bear it quietly and get back home.'

That was the last time Ponna had visited them. Seerayi had still gone there from time to time. And now she went there because she needed to inform them about the meeting and about Ponna's pregnancy—and she also wanted some of her people there to stand by her. Her first brother yelled at her, 'It was only for your sake that we even came when Kali died. He had taken her side and had stopped visiting us. How much more can we uncles keep doing? That woman spoke too much, but she still gets to have her way.'

'Water does not part simply because you beat it with a stick, da,' said Seerayi. 'Why do we need to keep talking about who said what and who was more in the wrong. It happened. I admit that she does speak impulsively. If the two bullocks locked to a cart pull in different directions, how can we get anywhere? They have said that there should be a few relatives present at the village council meeting. And who else have I got but you? I am asking you as an older sister. It will add to my respect if you come and stand there by my side. It will also dignify you. But I leave it to you. Do as you please.'

Even though these visits were only to inform people about the forthcoming meeting, Seerayi was still anxious that someone might say something harsh. Over the past week, she had vaguely heard some spiteful opinions. Apparently, one or two people were saying, 'They did not have a child until now. How did it happen now? How come the husband died just when a child was about to come? There is more to this. Ponna is not an innocent girl. She is capable of anything. She has done something. And Kali must have found out about it; and because he could not stand the shame of it, he hung himself.' There were also people who brought these bits of gossip to Seerayi, framing it as other people's opinions. Then there were those who had themselves witnessed Ponna going to the festival in a cart.

Seerayi heard that someone had said, 'If a woman over forty goes to the festivities, it might be an innocent thing. But when a young woman goes, it can't be for no reason. She must surely have gone to conceive a child. And it looks like the husband did not like that. Not all husbands accept this, do they? There are one or two men whose pride is wounded by this. This is not Kali's child; this is the temple festival's child.' Seerayi did not dignify any of these insinuations with a response. Rather, she addressed these comments in a very generic way. All she said was, 'What can I say? It is our fate that we endure this. Women who go to other men blatantly seem to face no troubles. But we have to bear these opinions. There is a god who bears witness to all this. He will take care of us.'

But since she wanted to make sure nothing untoward and difficult came to pass at the meeting, she was busy garnering support. She even spoke to Thorattu Paatti, saying, 'All of you came the other day and spoke words of comfort. It gave some strength to our minds. But people don't seem to want us to be happy. I hear that they are saying all sorts of things. Aaya, if all of you come to the village meeting, it will give us some strength. I know that usually women don't go to these meetings. But this is to do with the lives of two women. It will be good if all of us women stick together. We can guard against other people's nasty opinions.'

And Thorattu Paatti said to her, 'I too have heard these things, Seerayi. You don't worry, be brave. There are some five or six of us old women in the village. What are we good for? We will come to the meeting. Instead of sitting around in our homes, we will go and sit at the meeting. And we will get there early. You don't worry, go attend to your things.'

Muthu had asked Seerayi, 'Atthai, why are you going to so many places and inviting so many people? Wouldn't it be enough if just some four people show up for us?'

Seerayi had just smiled at this remark, and had not shared her apprehensions with him.

EIGHTEEN

The fact that there was still a week to go before the meeting helped Ponna find some courage. In the meantime, she also found a lot of support. At night, she would lie down, deep in thought. She felt strengthened by all the people who visited her and even this place that still reminded her of Kali. And Ponna's own movements, which had earlier been confined closer to the barnyard, now extended all over the field. She resolved to herself that the field was her responsibility from then on. That resolve made her happy. The very next day, early in the morning, Muthu brought a worker, Sengaan, with him. The day before, Muthu had sowed maize in the smaller square of land and had turned the soil over. That morning, he weeded out the kolunji from another land, sowed maize and ploughed the area. Sengaan busied himself with plucking away the kolunji in another square.

There was nothing more to do in the fields. The gap between the fields were wide enough for a cow to graze.

They were smooth and had no bumps or rocks. If one just held on to the rope and let the cow walk down the border of the field, the animal could walk and graze freely. The field itself was even, with no rock or stone to impede the movement of a plough or to trip a person walking there. Kali had sieved the soil carefully and had made sure it was of a fine texture. And the different squares of land were arranged in such a way that they gradually sloped down one after the other—the height difference between one piece of land and another being not more than the length of a finger. Within each piece of land, the soil was evenly spread out so that when it rained, the water would seep down wherever it fell. And if it rained considerably enough to have some standing water, the rainwater stood evenly all over the field, and would then overflow on to the next field without eroding any sand.

It was mostly red soil in all the fields. But in some parts, it appeared blackened. When Muthu examined it, he saw that the blackening was caused by manure mixing with the soil. Kali had not wasted any dung, refuse, leaves or stalks and had turned them into manure and mixed them inseparably with the soil. This would make sure that the soil would be fertile for four or five years. Even though Kali owned only four acres of land, because he took such good care of it, he always had a good harvest and made some extra cash. He never hesitated to go the extra mile. That was why Kali had spent as much as he did on the various rituals and offerings associated with praying for a child. Muthu felt that such a well-kept land would be a pleasure to work on. But then he immediately wondered if it was this perfectionism that had led to Kali's death. So what if things were a little imperfect? If a little stone halts the movement of a plough, you could always stop and remove it. And in that time it took to check if the edge of the plough had suffered any damage, the bulls could catch a moment of rest. And for the worker too, it would give a chance for the mind to settle briefly on something else for a change. He might call for some help. That would be a chance to have a short conversation. But on this plot of land, once he started ploughing, he could go on effortlessly till the end without any interruption.

Working on such a smooth stretch of land might actually be boring. Did Kali keep the land so clean because he wanted to keep people at a distance? There was not a single blemish on this land Kali had tended to. There was nothing lacking in the barnyard he had built. The water channel and plant beds were flawless. The picotah Kali had used to draw water worked perfectly. All the trees he had planted grew and thrived. None of his sheep and cattle were sick or weak. How could such a man accept any imperfection in his wife? Muthu was sad and surprised to realize that he had failed to understand this about a friend with whom he had spent so much time. But it occurred to him that Kali had not been like that when they were younger. It was only after the harshness of people's words drove him to the solitude of the barnyard that Kali must have gradually acquired this attitude of perfectionism.

Since they had missed ploughing the land in summer, Muthu now did it twice. So it took longer. By the time he was done with one field, he saw that Sengaan had removed kolunji from the entire field and was now gathering them and bundling them up. He quietly admired Sengaan's abilities as a worker. He then released the bulls from the plough, took them to the shade and gave them some water and food. After that, he drank some leftovers and got ready to leave. He said to Vallayi, 'Amma, I am going back to our village. Sengaan is here. He will do the rest of the ploughing. I will be back tomorrow in the morning.' Ponna was awake and she was sitting drinking coffee after rinsing her mouth. Muthu had still not started speaking directly to Ponna. He was afraid that she might respond harshly if he did. So he decided to let her make the first move. When Sengaan got ready to plough the rest of the land, Ponna walked over the field and sat in the shade of the palai tree that was next to the well.

From there, she had a clear view of the entire field. Now that the kolunji plants had been removed, it spread out like a stage set for action. The plough stood at the corner piece of the land that was to the east. Ponna recollected that it was on that land that she had planted the portia stalk, which Seerayi had then pulled out and flung away, and where Ponna had then placed a smooth stone to mark the spot. Now she was anxious that Sengaan not plough over that spot. She got up slowly and walked towards there. The sun was harsh. In such heat, the soil would retain moisture only for a day. Will they be able to do all the sowing and ploughing in one day? If they can't, they will have to wait for the next rain. When Sengaan saw Ponna approaching the field, he said, 'Why are you walking out in this heat?'

Sengaan had been labouring in Muthu's lands for several years. He was particularly affectionate towards Ponna. She now walked to that piece of land in the eastern corner and looked for the stone. 'There is a deity in this corner. I just wanted to make sure you don't plough it down,' she said. The stone glistened from the soil that was now free of weeds. It had taken on the hue of the red earth. And that was the corner where two adjacent squares of land met. Kali had made that intersection wide, so when they brought the cattle out to graze, they could sit there comfortably. Some palai plants had grown right behind the stone. They must have come up several days ago, and they showed the mark of resilience, of coming up from the roots no matter how often they were cut. Ponna thought she might let one of these plants grow big. She asked Sengaan to plough away from the little portion of land there. He said, 'Go back to the shade, dear child. I will take care of it.'

But Ponna had things to say to Sengaan. 'We have some water in the well. We can plant some chilli and tomato. And ragi in one field. We will only need to water it once a week. By next year, I will be able to draw water myself and irrigate the fields. This year, you or my brother please come and take care of that. Let us not sow maize everywhere.

We also cannot plant kambu any more. So it must be ragi. That's what will feed us.' She had spoken hurriedly.

'All right, dear. We shall do just as you say. We can leave out the brinjal bed and the bigger piece of land next to it for now. And in those stretches of land, we can do just as you just suggested. We might actually be able to finish all the maize sowing today. Keep coming to the field like this, my girl, then all your miseries will fly away just like the cotton-like flowers of that palai tree right there.' It was comforting to Ponna to listen to his words.

Since he had insisted, she walked back to the shade of the palai tree. Then she heard her mother call out to her from the barnyard—probably to eat. From now on, she had to eat for two beings. But she didn't have to get up right away; she could go in a little while. She felt that she may not have the strength to shout back to her mother from there. In just two days, Kali had sucked away all the strength from her body. She saw him in the tree. She saw him in the field. He had filled all these things, all these places, with himself. It was going to be an impossible task to be free of him. One more week. Then she had to stand in front of the village. What was she going to say? She could only declare that this child was indeed Kali's. He had come the night before and lain with her. He had the strength to take just one night to place in her a three-month-old foetus. And to accomplish that, he had put her through so much. He had just tucked his life away and kept it safe.

No. If it was three months, then it must have been the day Muthu had come to invite them to the temple festival. Kali had come home and knocked on the door in the middle of the night. She could recognize it was him from the knock. She opened the door and said, 'My brother is visiting you. Can't you stay away one night? What will he think?' But he took her in an embrace and said, 'Your brother is sleeping soundly where I've left him. Not even thunder can wake him up now. Whereas I could not sleep thinking of you.' She could count the days from that night. Kali had laid his head on her chest and dozed off. She had then woken him up and sent him back to the barnyard. She had been anxious, wondering what her brother would think if he woke up and found that Kali was gone. Kali had been reluctant to leave even after she had woken him up. She had to push him out of the house and bolt the door from the inside. Even if she had to think of this child as growing in her womb since the last day of the festival, the fact was that on that day she had not been able to stop thinking about Kali for even a second.

Attempting to avoid being reminded of Kali, she had turned down and moved away from several men. But he had been there even in that one chest against which she had finally reclined that night. She had seen him when she closed her eyes; she had seen him when she opened her eyes. Since she could not do anything about it, she had just embraced him with all her heart. Then how could anyone say this child was not his? Even Kali had no right to say that. She would say out loud in front of the village, even to the entire world: 'This life growing in me was given by Kali.' Now she felt very bold. Seerayi was running around and inviting people as if she was inviting them to a wedding. The night before, Seerayi and Vallayi had made a list of all the people who needed to be invited, and the people whom they should insist ought to come to the meeting. Ponna's grandfather's name too featured in that list. But Ponna did not need anyone. Now she could boldly speak. She lay down in the shade of the palai tree.

She lay there as if she was lying on Kali's lap.

NINETEEN

It was a moonlit night that Saturday. Only Seerayi and Vallayi were with Ponna. As they had become accustomed to having some visitor or another staying the night and keeping them company, on nights such as this one, when it was just the three of them, they really felt like something was missing.

Ponna was struggling with morning sickness. As the day would progress, she somehow found ways to manage. Even earlier that day, she had gone over to the fields and returned to the barnyard only after several hours. It had been as if she was seeing the entire expanse of the fields properly for the first time. It was only now that she was getting to know the different sections of this land. Some sections of the land even came to her as surprises. Looking at the various things, she could not but wonder what Kali would have done with them and what she could do with them now.

It would take her a while to fall asleep each night despite the exhaustion; she would sleep late into the morning. If the portia tree moved or if the dog barked, she would start wondering if Kali was paying her a visit again. In fact, she eagerly looked forward to his visit, but she was not sure he would come again. His job had been done. Perhaps that had been the very purpose of this three-month-long mourning period. But even if he did not come again, he must still be lingering somewhere nearby. He might be the crow that flew around in the fields. He might be able to see everything. Only she was not able to see him. She would lie in her cot, thinking of him. Outside the hut, Seerayi and Vallayi would be murmuring something to each other. They might be talking of people who still needed to be invited to the meeting.

Ponna was not thrilled with the fact that Seerayi went to her brothers' and invited them all. But Seerayi said, 'They think we have come down in the world. Don't we have to let them know that we are, in fact, rising up again? That's why I went.' Well, if doing that helped Seerayi find some peace, then good for her. Ponna had resolved that she would not say anything harsh to Seerayi. 'I have suffered one loss,' she thought to herself, 'but Seerayi has suffered two: first a husband and then a son.'

The dog barked suddenly, sensing some movement in the alley beside the fence. Seerayi got up to see what it was, saying, 'This dog starts barking even if a garden lizard moves.' But she heard sounds of people approaching. Then she heard someone call out 'Saami . . .' over the noise of the dog's barking. 'Who is there?' Seerayi called out and walked towards the thatched gate.

'It is me, Kaaraan,' came the response. 'I thought this might be a convenient time to come and talk to you, saami.'

'Yes, yes, come,' Seerayi welcomed him. He had brought his wife and daughter-in-law along with him. 'Kaaraan, have all of you eaten?' Seerayi asked. They had.

Seerayi and Vallayi had roasted some peanuts earlier that evening for Ponna. There were some left. Seerayi gave a handful to each of the visitors. Bundling his share of nuts in his towel, Kaaraan said, 'It was I who went to Adaiyur the other day to convey the news of our landlady's pregnancy. Her brother, Muthu, dropped me back in their cart. He asked me to find a woman labourer to help in the fields here. That's what I have come to talk about.'

Seerayi said, 'Oh, is that so? He did not tell us anything about that. We don't seem to have enough work to hire someone for.'

Vallayi joined in. 'He did not say anything to me either. Maybe he was just making small talk. But I will speak to him tomorrow and get back to you, all right?'

Kaaraan looked deflated. He had come with hope, and now he did not know how to respond. He was also afraid of how his wife and daughter-in-law might react.

Ponna got up from her bed, stepped outside the hut and sat down on the stone. The visitors were sitting a little away, on the ground. She said, 'Brother might have said that for a reason. He must have thought it through. And he might have forgotten to tell us this among his various errands.'

Seerayi replied, 'All right, but are we in a position now to hire help for the fields?'

But Ponna knew that her mother Vallayi was already anxious to go back to her village. She was just waiting for the third month of mourning and observances to end. There was a lot of work back home that she needed to get back to. Ponna's sister-in-law could not handle everything single-handedly. And they were also considering the possibility of taking Ponna with them there, keeping her with them for seven months. Muthu must have thought of all this and the fact that Seerayi could not manage the sheep and cattle on her own here. Ponna had no plans to go with her mother to her village. Her plan was to deliver the child right here in the barnyard so that Kali could hear the child's sounds from the portia tree. Besides, she could take care of these fields only if she stayed here. So it would be good to have help.

She addressed Kaaraan, 'Who will be that person? Your wife or your daughter-in-law?'

He replied, 'My daughter-in-law, saami. She has three children. My son works in the field whenever he finds work. But whatever he earns, he spends on toddy. How can they feed the children? My wife and I are here for now to take care of them. But it will be hard as they grow older. My wife says she will take care of the children if my daughter-in-law can go out to work. The kids are small. If they are fed some gruel, they will spend their time playing around.

Let my daughter-in-law come and work here in the field. It will at least help us feed ourselves.'

'You say she has little children,' said Seerayi. 'Will she be able to come to work properly? It does not look like this will work out, Kaaraan.'

But Ponna thought otherwise. She felt it was a good arrangement. Karaan's daughter-in-law had come the previous year to help with ragi harvesting. She had worked quietly and had not wasted time in useless chit-chat. Nor had she stolen any grains in the folds of her sari. She had even come forward to lift and carry the basket in which the harvested produce was collected. It was clear that she was a hard worker. That was enough. And if she could not come to work for a day or two because she had to attend to her children, that was all right by Ponna. So she said, 'Oh, she can do it. What do you say, Venga? You should be diligent with work. Women run this farm. If you can't be regular, it won't work out.'

Vengayi stood up immediately and said, 'I will definitely come regularly, saami. My daughter is seven years old. She will take care of all the chores in the house. The boy will be five soon. After a year, I will send him out to herd sheep for someone. And the youngest is a girl, she is three. She is able to drink the leftover rice by herself. But if she needs me, I can bring her here, let her play here somewhere, and I can keep working.'

Seerayi considered a lot of things and came to the conclusion that this would be a good arrangement. She also realized that it would be a struggle for her without some help. Vallayi, for her part, thinking this would be a good time to speak, said, 'This is a good idea, because I will need to go back home soon too. There is a lot of work waiting for me there. After all, how can Poovayi handle everything on her own?' Then she addressed Vengayi and said, 'Agree on a wage, and be reliable with your work.'

Seerayi said, 'All right. Can you come tomorrow? We can talk further when Muthu is here.'

But Ponna said, 'No need for all that. Let us decide right away. Kaaraan, what wage do you expect? Ask as per the norms in the village. Ours is a small farm, so the work too will be proportional to that. We are not the sort of people who say one thing now and then go back on our word. So ask.' Kaaraan replied, 'It is nothing that you don't know about. A woman labourer is given two pots of dried grains, and a sari each for Pongal and the chariot festival. Other than that, you could give whatever groundnuts or grams you have. I am sure you will do the right thing.'

'Two pots of grains is a lot, Kaaraan,' said Seerayi.

'Please don't say that. That's what we depend on for our food,' said Kaaraan.

Ponna immediately said, 'All right. Atthai, it is only for little kids to eat. So let us do that. Kaaraan, we will give you what you have asked for. But please make sure she does not miss workdays because you have to visit relatives and all that. Things have to be proper. They say that farms run by women don't thrive. We don't want to prove them right.'

Vengayi, who was still standing, said, 'My work will please you, saami.' In the moonlight, Ponna could see that Vengayi was bringing her hands together in a gesture of respect.

Karaan's wife stood up and said, 'She is my brother's daughter, saami. She will conduct herself well. You please take care of us. We depend on you.'

At this, Seerayi said to Vallayi, 'Sister, please bring a measure of ragi from inside.'

But Karaan's wife said, referring to Ponna, 'She is pregnant. Let her give us the grains with her own hand.' What she said made Ponna very happy. She walked back into the hut.

She heard Seerayi's say, 'It is the month of Aadi now. We calculate the year from Chithirai. So it will be three months short of a full year. And we will pay you accordingly.' Ponna came out carrying some kambu millets and poured it in the fold of Vengayi's sari. She then asked, 'Will you start tomorrow?'

Kaaraan replied, 'Please excuse her just for tomorrow. We have a hen, and we are thinking of making an offering of it tomorrow. Let her start from the day after. It is also a Monday.'

Ponna duly agreed, feeling satisfied with these developments.

TWENTY

By the time Ponna was awake, Vengayi had already arrived for work. It was well into the morning.

Ponna thought about her craving for hot rice. They cooked rice just for her these days for all three meals. But she felt that she shouldn't be eating luxuriously like this for too long. There was some rice in the gifts that came from her father's family. But she knew that she had to keep that away for a rainy day. Besides, everyone was saying her morning sickness would go away in a month. Sometimes, she touched her tummy and felt around it inquisitively, but she could not make out anything yet. All she knew was that she was easily hungry and irritable. Perhaps the life that was growing inside her demanded food. Perhaps it was this little life that spoke in annoyance through her. But she also didn't feel like eating just about anything; she had specific cravings.

She was amazed to find out how skilful one's nose was. The tongue seemed to reject anything the nose did not prefer. Even if the leftover rice had gone just a tad sour, the nose deduced it even from a distance. It also seemed to take in very distant smells, like it was a dog's nose. Even the stench of cow dung and sheep refuse had grown in intensity. She was simply unable to bear the foul smell of the dog. And it became impossible for her to eagerly open the rice pot and look into it. The fragrance was so sharp that it felt like a slap on her face. It felt like she had no control over her body. She had to let it lead her wherever it would.

Seerayi could not think of anything other than the village meeting that loomed ahead. Ponna tried to calm her by saying, 'Atthai, what can they do? Don't worry. No one will accuse us.' But nothing soothed Seerayi's anxieties.

A few nights ago, after finalizing the arrangements with Vengayi, Seerayi had walked to the gate to shut it behind Kaaraan, his wife and Vengayi. Just then, Kaaraan had said, 'We have some relatives in Pazhayur. I ran into them at the market the other day, and we got talking. We were meeting after several years. They told me that they got to ride in our Muthu's bullock cart to the festival. When I told them about what had happened to Kali, they expressed sadness that such misfortunes happened to good people.'

Seerayi listened to this calmly, but later she asked Vallayi, 'Did you give anyone a ride on your way to the temple festival?' Vallayi then told her about how they had given a lift to a family of four: husband, wife and two children. The man's name was Maaran or something like that. He was adept at handling bulls. Ponna still vividly remembered the child's face.

'It turns out that he is related to Kaaraan,' said Seerayi, agitated. 'Looks like he has asked after us.'

Ponna said, 'When we travel somewhere, a thousand people will see us. We can't think of everyone and keep feeling afraid.'

But Seerayi's worries could not be pacified. Ponna felt that Seerayi would calm down only once the meeting was over, but she was also a little anxious that in her state of agitation, Seerayi might disclose too much to someone. She had taken the whole thing very seriously.

It made Ponna happy just to look at Vengayi's face. She was so radiant. She must be only twenty-five or twenty-six years old. She had used castor oil on her head and had combed it down neatly. And she wore a chain of black beads around her neck. Teasing her on her prim and proper appearance, Ponna said, 'Are you sure you have come to work in the fields?' Vengayi laughed.

Vallayi shouted after her, 'Ponna, please don't do any work yourself.'

Ponna replied sarcastically, 'I will just sit in the shade. We will just live off the food that comes from your house in the cart.' She was carrying a basket which she had picked up just before setting out. But Vengayi took the basket from her right away. Vallayi was not at all offended by Ponna's remark. On the contrary, it made her happy that the spark was back in Ponna's voice now.

Just like she said she would, Ponna sat in the shade of the palai tree. The day's task was to make a sand bed right next to the brinjal patch and plant chilli in one quarter of that bed and ragi in half of it. Vengayi worked with a spade. It looked like there had been a plant bed there earlier. So she worked within that. Ponna marvelled at how tirelessly Vengayi dug the sand out. She was not distracted by anything and just kept at her work. Once she had finished digging and built the raised bed, Ponna called out to her and asked her to go drink some water in the barnyard and also bring some for her. Vengayi complied, and brought a pitcher of water on her return. She did not tell Ponna that Vallayi had teasingly asked her, 'Did your landlady send you for something?' Ponna sent Vengayi again to the barnyard, this time to bring some dried cow dung. It took Vengayi a little longer to return. Since Vallayi was alone in the barnyard, she was bored and had caught hold of Vengayi for a chat.

Vengayi crumbled the dried cow dung, spread it on the sand bed and made sure it mixed well with the soil. Then Ponna asked her to sow the chilli and ragi seeds with just enough space for the saplings to grow well. Vengayi said, 'For good luck, perhaps you could sow some seeds with your own hands.'

That set off a lament from Ponna. 'But look at me, I am draped in white now. From now on, they will say it is unlucky to start a day looking at my face. They will turn away if they see me coming down the street. They will say I should not take part in auspicious functions. Do you think they will include me in anything from now on? No. Earlier, they pushed me away because I was childless. Now even though I have a child on the way, they will shun me because I am a widow. Look what my life has become, Venga. I cannot take the lead and take part in anything any more. He has left me in this state.'

Vengayi said, 'Saami, people say that women in white are like the goddess. Please think of that. You are pregnant now. If you sow the seeds with your own hands, they will be blessed and will grow well.'

'That is as far as respect for this white sari will go,' Ponna replied, 'and not any further. Just like that deity stays confined to the temple, I will be made to limit my movements to the barnyard. As it is, women are restricted mostly to the house and the front yard. But now, I don't have even that. I can't even go stand at the gate . . . You plant it yourself, Venga. It will grow well. You have given birth to three children.'

Vengayi started sowing the seeds, saying with sadness, 'What is there in a sari? You could just wear a coloured sari. In our community, they don't insist on these things any more.'

'You people even get married after you are widowed,' replied Ponna. 'You even say that women can marry however many times they want, just like men do. But look at my situation here. I am required to go stand in front of a lot of people and declare that this child growing in my womb is indeed my husband's. I am expected to do this in front of men who wander as they please—just like dogs that would lick even what's thrown in the trash. And these are the men who will deal out justice. Do you have any such thing in your community? Tell me.' It had been months since Ponna had spoken like this. Somehow, she felt the urge to speak to Vengayi.

'In our community,' said Vengayi, 'they say a woman should not stay widowed. My mother's younger sister's son got married just last month. His father had died some five or six years ago. She was a widow all these years and lived by herself. What was she going to do with a husband at that age? But they said she needed a husband to take part in all the wedding rituals for her son. So my father put a pottu on her forehead and married her. In front of several witnesses at a temple, he took vermilion in his hands and marked her forehead with it. That was the wedding. Then my father and she performed all the wedding rituals for her son. This is how we poor people do things. It is people like you who are concerned about so many things.'

Ponna was pleasantly surprised that Vengayi was so talkative. When she had first seen Vengayi the year before at the ragi harvest, she had given the impression that she was a quiet worker. But even now, Vengayi's hands kept working without a break. Ponna sighed. 'It is not as if we are well-to-do people. All we have is this land. That is all. What else do these people have? Fucking nothing! But they have a ton of pride for sure.' Her words came out in anger.

Vengayi was a little taken aback and also unsure if Ponna's anger was directed at her or at the world in general. She wondered if she had said anything that might have hurt Ponna. But Ponna cleared up these confusions when she soon resumed the conversation casually. She came closer to observe Vengayi sowing the seeds, and said, 'You are really good at your work. Now all that remains to be done is to water this bed. My brother will be here soon. I will ask him to lock the bullocks to the picotah and draw water.'

Vengayi replied, 'Why go to all that trouble for this little patch? All it needs is some five or six pots of water.'

Ponna said, 'But who will do it? I can't do it in this state. I'd ask you to help, but my mother and mother-in-law will definitely object. We can do it the usual way.'

Ponna saw that the brinjal plants had some tender new shoots. She had previously asked Muthu to plough and ready those sections of the field where they intended to transfer the chilli and ragi saplings once the seeds sprouted and grew. When Muthu and Sengaan arrived for that task, they could also draw water and irrigate this patch. All the squares of land where they had sown maize looked dusty now. There was a long, narrow piece of land beyond, and Ponna had asked them not to sow anything there. This land bordered the common pathway beyond the fence. She thought this might be a good place to let the cattle graze and to keep them tethered during the day. Vengayi brought a few dried coconut fronds that were lying under the coconut tree, and laid them over the bed in which she had sowed the seeds today. If the sun fell directly on the bed, the soil might dry and wilt, and the seeds may not sprout. Observing Vengayi as she went about her tasks responsibly, often taking the initiative to go the extra mile without being asked to, Ponna felt convinced about Vengayi's work ethic. This also enhanced her confidence in the possibility of running this farm with Vengayi's assistance alone.

On their walk back to the barnyard, Ponna said, 'Venga, please don't address me as "saami". Nor as "lady". Just call me "Ponnu". That will do.'

'But people might find that objectionable, Ponnu,' Vengayi said and laughed.

Ponna too joined in Vengayi's merriment, laughing and saying, '"Ponnu" is respectful enough. No one will say anything.'

Ponna had laughed quite a bit that day.

TWENTY-ONE

They were counting the days to the meeting. When you are anxious about something, the days leading up to it, the days of preparing for it, become far more important than the actual day of reckoning. Those days are full of anxiety, pain, sorrow, anticipation, fear and so on. And they cause much excitement too. But nothing really helps us get past those days. The greatest consolation is that they do eventually come to pass. People spend that time in various ways. Seerayi, for one, had become convinced that her entire family's chances to see better days depended on the outcome of the meeting. Ponna's plan was simply to take charge of the farm work. As for Vallayi, she was eager to be done with the village meeting—and also the stipulated period of mourning—so that she could finally head back to her own village. She had been feeling more confident about leaving now that Vengayi was here to help. Perhaps Vallayi could come once every two or three days and stay over for the night. She might also cook food and bring some along.

The village meeting had to go smoothly. Seerayi could focus on nothing but counting down the days. On Tuesday night, she said to no one in particular, 'Wednesday, Thursday. Two days left.'

'And what happens after that?' came a voice from outside. 'You go and join your son in heaven?'

The dog did not bark at the visitor. Sensing that it was Nallayyan Uncle who was arriving, Seerayi said teasingly, 'Looks like I did not shut the gate properly. Some dog is walking in. Go shut it properly, akka,' as if she were addressing Vallayi.

Nallayyan walked in, ready with his rejoinder. 'No one can chase this dog away. It will go when it chooses to.'

He lay down on one of the cots, but Seerayi continued to tease him: 'Looks like my brother-in-law is very tired. Must be all the children he has to take care of. So much work!'

Nallayyan had never married. He had two younger brothers. He had taken his portion of inheritance and lived on his own. He roamed around as he pleased, often returning to the village after a week or even a month. Sometimes he brought some woman with him; he usually sent her away after a while. He did not care at all about what the village or the family had to say. Nallayyan was a paternal kinsman—and Kali was his agnate. He had always been very fond of Kali. He would come and stay in the barnyard every now and then when Kali had been around. And he was always one to chat away happily. Spending time with him invariably had the effect of lightening one's worries. Ponna loved listening to him. She now stepped out of the hut and welcomed him.

'My dear daughter-in-law,' he said. 'Looks like Kali has given you a child, but he was not lucky enough to stay and enjoy this blessing.'

She stood silently.

'Some people are like that,' continued Nallayyan. 'They don't know when to live and when to die. They die when they are supposed to live. And when it's time to die, they weep, seeking to hold on to life. We should neither be afraid to live nor die. Each ought to be given the time it is due . . . I have tried to tell him these things so many times. It looks like my words never reached beyond his ears. He never took them to heart. All right, he did not have to listen to me—but couldn't he think for himself either?'

As she stood listening to him, Ponna could not hold back her tears. This man knew everything about her husband. Kali used to say that talking to Nallayyan Uncle comforted him. He would say, 'I want to live like my uncle, my chithappa. But I am unable to. It takes a different mental attitude to live like him.' Ponna pressed the end of her sari to her mouth, trying hard to control her sobs.

'Don't cry, my girl,' comforted Nallayyan. 'What will crying accomplish? It is not going to bring him back, is it? We should live happily in the little time that we are here. What can we do about someone who does not understand what happiness is and chooses to go away. We can't hold him back. I was here that day. I am a man who sees quite a bit of the world, but even I could not bear the sorrow of his death. That was when it occurred to me that perhaps I had considered him my own son. I did not cry that much even when my parents died. I cried so much for this stupid dog. Everyone was fond of him. There was no one who did not like Kali. Everyone in the village knows how much you loved him. And your mother-in-law? He was her entire world. What about your brother? He rolled on the floor, sobbing and wailing, "I only wanted what was best for you! Why did you do this?" That was the first time I ever saw a man bawling like that. How many men get such a loving brother-in-law? Who else? Your parents, Ponna? Did they not like him? Or me? Or anyone in the village? Everyone liked Kali. But he did not know how much everyone liked him. Life is all about living with people we like, living for people we like. Why care about what the village says—the people out there who do not matter at all. The village has a stinking mouth that reeks of shit even when it is opened to yawn. It's even worse when that mouth is opened to speak. Why should we become victims of that? Anyway, he has given you a child. That is a small blessing. Raise this child and be happy. Give us a boy. I will bequeath my wealth to this boy, this grandson of mine.'

Ponna spoke softly, 'I want a girl child, Uncle. If it is a boy, he wouldn't think twice about deserting a woman in this manner, leaving her to suffer alone.'

He replied, 'It doesn't matter if it is a boy or a girl. The thing is, in our communities, a girl child has to endure a lot. It is a little easier on the boys. That's what I'd really meant. A boy has claims over not just this house and these fields, but the entire world, really. He can go wherever he wants, whenever he chooses. Ask your mother-in-law if she could control Kali's movements. Here, men are able to do what they want wherever they are. That is not the case with women. They have to stay tied to a particular place. They can't even let their eyes wander. When we tie a rope muzzle on a calf, it can't do much. It's the same thing with people. A man can even marry another woman if his wife dies. Or he can just keep a woman. Or go to them when he pleases. But look at your plight. They have given you a white sari. I think we should appeal to the white man and have this practice of the white sari banned. Your lot now is to wear this sari and just stay confined to this place. Can you marry another man? Will you ever have the courage to do that? A woman's life involves sacrificing everything and staying within very narrow bounds. That is why I asked you to give birth to a boy. So that the child could have some happiness. But if it is a girl child that you want, so be it.'

Seerayi spoke now. 'It is going to be an only child. We need it to be a boy for this line to last. If it is a girl, she will eventually have to go to another family.'

Vallayi agreed. 'Yes. And once you marry off your daughter, your worries still don't end. Look at us now. If it is a boy, he can just live where he is.'

'Sister-in-law,' said Nallayyan, 'is it only a man who ensures the continuation of a family line? A woman does not? And what is this family and lineage anyway? Do crows have a lineage? Do sparrows have a lineage? Why do men alone need a lineage, an heir and all that? All the lives that are born in the world are the same. We are born, we live, we die. That is all there is to it. All right, let me ask you this, sister-in-law. You speak about the importance of the family line. What was your father's name?'

'You know his name,' said Seerayi. 'My father's name was Sonaan.'

'And what was your grandfather's name?'

'My grandfather. Of course, I know his name. He was alive until I was an adolescent. His name was Marappan or something.'

'All right. What was your great-grandfather's name?'

'Who remembers their great-grandfather's name? Why are you asking me all this now? It is hard enough to remember what happened yesterday.'

'You can't even recollect your paternal great-grandfather's name,' reasoned Nallayyan. 'That's what will happen to your name too. Think about it. Do you think your great-grandson will know your name? Lineage, it seems!'

'Ah!' exclaimed Seerayi. 'Can I ever win an argument with you? We are merely taking the path that people have laid out over the ages. But you refuse to follow that path! You insist you will make a new one.'

Nallayyan turned to speak to Vallayi too. He said, 'If it is a girl, she can wear new saris. She can visit her parents for

169

a few days, stay with them. She will cook chicken and puttu for you. And when we die, the girl will come to sit near our heads and cry for us. A boy, on the other hand, will stand outside and quietly shed tears into his towel.'

Seerayi sighed. 'It sounds good when you put it like that. But that's not how everyone thinks, is it? We are just trying to fit in.'

'Anyway,' said Nallayyan decisively, 'let's not talk about that any more. I hear that you have called for a meeting to make an announcement to the village. I hear you have been inviting everyone. How come you haven't invited me?'

Seerayi explained, 'I did go to your house to invite you. You weren't there. I spoke to the worker boy. He said he did not know where you had gone and when you would come back.'

'So,' he asked, 'did all the wives in the village conceive their children only with their respective husbands? Can they prove that to the entire village?'

'If they leave it up to you, you will declare that all the women in the village are whores.'

'All right, then. Tell me, are they all chaste wives?'

'I am not saying anything. Who cares what other women do!'

'All of you talk about how I have not married and have no children. But if you really count, there are some five or six children in this very village who are born to me, do you know?' He laughed.

Seerayi retorted, 'Oh, then divide your wealth among them.'

'I am ready to do that, but their mothers don't agree. What can I do?'

'Oh, brother-in-law! What are you trying to say? How can we go against the village norms and continue to live here!'

'All right,' he said. 'Don't fret. I too will come to the meeting. If they see me there, the men will hesitate to speak. And if they do, I will handle it.'

'Sure, do come,' said Seerayi, before proceeding to elaborate on her worries. 'But speak carefully. Otherwise, they will speak ill of you too. Already, people are saying all sorts of spiteful things, as if they saw everything with their own eyes. All I want is to go inform people at this meeting that the child is Kali's and just be done with it so that we can get on with our lives!'

Nallayyan said calmly, 'The people of this village are scared of me. I will make use of that fact. You wait and see what I do.'

'All right,' said Seerayi. 'Tell me this. We have not seen you in a long time. Where did you go?'

Nallayyan Uncle was an expert at narrating anecdotes from his wanderings. Ponna sat down on the stone, eager to listen to his stories.

The breeze that moved the portia tree was gentle.

TWENTY-TWO

'I am now scared for my life, sister-in-law,' whispered Nallayyan Uncle fearfully. 'Even when I am back in the village, I work in the fields during the day and run away somewhere else for the night. Tonight, I plan to stay right here. Whenever I came here while Kali was alive, I used to wonder if I would ever have a place like this. But what is the use of simply desiring something? Who can work and make a place like Kali did? It is sad that he did not get to live and enjoy this for long. But even now, even when he is not here any more, this place is still protecting me. There are three men looking for me. They want to kill me. Even if I spend a single night at my place, they will definitely kill me.'

Ponna wondered if Nallayyan Uncle was losing his mind. She also wondered if this was the result of Uncle coveting some woman and incurring the anger of her family. Perhaps that was why these men were after him.

'A man is not born yet who can kill you,' Seerayi said. 'You are speaking like a madman.'

Uncle went on, 'It is my youngest brother and his two sons who are after me. Apparently, they are saying that they don't even care if one of them has to go to prison, that they will make sure they murder me. I didn't keep quiet. I filed a complaint with the local authorities. I told them my brother and his sons were keen on killing me and that if anything were to happen to me, they should be put in jail.'

Seerayi asked, 'Why are they after your wealth now? You are hale and hearty, strong enough to marry two women. What's their hurry?'

'I don't know,' he said, sounding frustrated. 'Both those boys are after my property. I am sick and tired of this. I feel like selling it all and going away somewhere.'

When they had divided up the inheritance, Nallayyan Uncle had claimed one-third of it. Even back then, his brothers had tried all they could to acquire his share for themselves. At first they had cajoled and wheedled—they had competed with each other in taking care of him, feeding him, pampering him with food and snacks. He had thought he should enjoy all the attention while it lasted. But, of course, this did not last long as their devotion was false and they had eyes only on his share of the inheritance. When they eventually realized that he was not going to relent and offer them his share, they decided to change their tactics. The first brother had a son and two daughters—the son would inherit his father's full share, and so the only concern was finding suitable husbands for the daughters. But the youngest brother had two sons and two daughters—and thus the two sons would have to divide the wealth among themselves, each getting only half of what their father had inherited. Both these sons conspired with their father, and came to the conclusion that if they also managed to get their uncle's—that is Nallayyan's—share they would have enough between the two of them. And since they knew Nallayyan had a weakness for women, a plan was hatched: they sent their own mother to him.

One night, she came to his place bearing rice and chicken kuzhambu, and she also stayed back to serve him. Usually, she would just drop off the food and leave. And when she served him the food, everything from her conversation to her expressions seemed quite explicitly encouraging to him. She looked quite youthful despite being over forty and a mother of four. He had not experienced this kind of intimacy with her before. So, deciding to try his luck, he reached out and touched her. And she seemed to respond favourably. From then on, she came every week, with the full knowledge of her husband, sons and daughters. She would come late at night to his hut. As for Nallayyan, he was glad that he did not have to go looking for a woman; a woman was coming to him now. She grew quite fond of him. What started haltingly, perhaps once a week, soon became more frequent.

Nallayyan said, 'My brother, he works all day in the fields. At night, he fills his stomach with toddy, and he does not come back home. Just stays in the little hut in the fields. He has married off a daughter. The other girl is very young. The two sons are of marriageable age. And even if my brother did come home at night, he was clearly not of much use. When it rains on parched land, what happens? It sucks in everything, doesn't it? And that's what happened with her too. I am very experienced; I have been with many. So it did not take me long to figure out precisely what she craved for. And I must say, she was quite good. She would stand when I asked her to, sit when I told her to; she would even bend over if that's what I wanted. She did everything I desired. My brother married such a woman, but he could not live happily with her. What kind of a man is he?'

Seerayi, Vallayi and Ponna, all three of them laughed listening to this. Ponna found it difficult to contain her amusement. Seerayi said to Nallayyan, 'You have no decency, no shame. The things you say!'

'We should talk about these things, Seerayi,' he said. 'A man should ask a woman what she likes. Go see what happens in the prostitutes' street in Karattur. If they don't like a man, they hit him with a slipper and send him away.'

He then continued with the story. His brother's wife had started spending more and more time with him. When her husband or sons came looking for her, she sent them away, saying, 'Yes, yes, I will come. You go.' She had turned into a whole new person. She devoted her time cooking for him, working in his fields, chatting and laughing with him. She refused to leave even when he asked her to.

Thinking that she was being intimate with him only for his money, he had said, 'Should I will my inheritance to you or to your sons? Either way, my wealth goes to them after me.' And she had replied, 'It is true that they sent me to you with the intention of taking your share. And I too came to you at first with that idea. But now neither do I want your money, nor do I want to have anything to do with those wretched people. I will just stay here with you. That is all I want. I have not had a man as good as you. I cannot believe they speak so ill of you.'

But her husband, Nallayyan's brother, could not bear to see how openly his wife was flaunting her intimacy with Nallayyan. Once, he came to take her back. She said, 'I will come. You go.' But he was angry. He said, 'What is so special about him? Does he leak milk? Is that why you are so eager to receive him?' That provoked her. She said, 'Yes. Milk flows from his manhood. Unlike yours. You first try getting it up!' That was when the brother realized just how far this had gone. He pulled her by the hair, dealt her some blows on the back and dragged her home with him.

Even though Nallayyan had been scared after that incident, he had not made a big deal out of the matter, thinking that he could not be blamed for any of it. But then she returned to him that very night. Her younger son followed her and dragged her back home, muttering, 'She can't stay away even for a day.'

She had shouted, 'Let go of me! I gave birth to you. You think you can talk to me like this? When you thought you could get his share of the property, you were ready to do anything. How come you did not question your father that day when he was ready to send me on this errand? But here you are today! Your uncle has said he will leave this property to you. Isn't that what you wanted? Now let go of me. I will stay with him and spend the rest of my life here. I will be of no trouble to you. You don't have to take care of me. When I can't take care of myself any more, I will hang myself and die!'

It was night-time, and even the other brother's family could hear all that she had said. They had come by to see what was happening. But by then, the son had forcibly dragged his mother home with him. 'Let my husband question me!' she had yelled. 'I will answer him. Who are you to question me? You are manhandling your own mother? What kind of a man are you?' Enraged, her son then punched her right on her mouth. She went home with broken teeth and a bloodied mouth.

'Nothing serious,' Nallayyan had explained to his other brother, who had come to see what was going on. 'The husband and wife were arguing. She came here, asking me to intervene. So her son came over to take her back.' But his other brother did not believe him. He had said, 'I have been observing what's been going on. So he thinks he can send his wife to you and get you to give him your property? I cannot stoop so low. But if you give them your money just because she showed you this and that, I will cut your throat and go to jail.'

Alarmed, Nallayyan had said, 'This is my money. I will give it to whomever I want. Why are you fighting with me about it?' And his brother threatened, 'Half of it is mine. Remember that. If you do anything else, I will cut your throat, throw your body in the fields. I will tell everyone I don't know where you went, what happened to you.'

Listening to all this, Seerayi now asked Nallayyan, 'What did they do to the woman after they dragged her back home?'

'Oh, don't even ask,' he answered ominously as he rose from the cot.

The wind howled, growing agitated.

TWENTY-THREE

One could not pinpoint what it was about Nallayyan Uncle that his brother's wife found so irresistible. But she became completely besotted with him. Her husband and sons would hit her brutally and viciously abuse her as well. But she gave as good as she got. Then one morning, the family woke up to find that she was gone. They later heard that she was at Nallayyan's place, clearing out cow dung in the shed there. They decided to wait till she returned of her own accord. But it didn't look as though that was going to happen.

Fearful that all of this would get him into trouble, Nallayyan had tried reasoning with her. 'Look here,' he said. 'I understand that you have grown very fond of me. But you are not a woman I have brought from elsewhere. You are my brother's wife. You have married off one of your daughters, and you have three other children ready to be married. You are a family woman. Do you think it is right for you to leave them all and come and shack up here? Just come once or twice a week. We will spend time together. They may not object to that. But if you want to drop everything there and move here permanently, how will they accept that? Tell me. The people who come seeking marriage alliances with your family, if they find out what is going on here, will they ever approach your family? Only if we keep it all hush-hush can we carry on for a while. Go now.'

But she simply refused to budge. 'I don't even care to look at their faces any more,' she said decisively. 'Let them deal with things. They are calling me a prostitute now. But who sent me whoring in the first place? They did, didn't they? If they stand to get some property, they don't care if the wife becomes a whore. Your brother's pride is wounded now. He even says, "Tell me how my brother does it. I will do it the same way with you." Why didn't that occur to him earlier? I would rather die than go back there. I am even ready to bear a child for you. We can stay here and raise that child.'

Angered by this adamance, Nallayyan slapped her a few times and pushed her out of his house, saying, 'All of you— your entire family, husband, wife, sons—all of you have decided to torment me. I am not going to keep any woman with me. Now, go, run away! I will call you when I need you. You can come then. Go now!' But none of this had any effect on her. She just sat on the hard ground outside Nallayyan's home, staring at him. It made Nallayyan Uncle feel some pity towards her. She had everything—a husband, daughters, a family. Nor did she lack wealth. But there she was, sitting in front of him, like a beggar. He called her back in and gave her some food. 'If you can be there and also come here from time to time, I can agree to that. Otherwise, I don't want you. I don't have any ties here. I will drop everything as it is and go elsewhere.'

She told him she would do as he wished, and then returned home. But that night, when she tried to leave for his place again, the family stopped her and even beat her up. She tried to run away. But they tied her up inside the house. The next morning, she begged and pleaded with her daughter, who was doing all the housework by herself. Overcome with pity, the daughter untied her, saying, 'Amma, why are you acting like this at your age? It is so shameful. If people in the village find out, we will never be able to hold our heads high ever again.' For a little while, she stayed there, helping her daughter with the domestic chores. But then she suddenly vanished. When they looked for her, they saw her walking across the adjacent field towards Nallayyan's house. Realizing that this was never going to end, they dragged her towards a bullock cart and took her to her father's village in Seeroor.

They decided to let her stay there for a while until things calmed down. She had a big family—father, mother, elder brother, younger brother. They also had a large farm. They took turns keeping watch over her. For three days, she stayed there, mostly sitting as if she was in a daze. But somehow she left on the third night and came to Nallayyan's house. He could not turn her away since she had come to his door in the dead of the night.

'What could I do?' Nallayyan said despondently. 'I took her in and gave her some food. She ate as if she had not eaten in days. At her parents' place, they would surely have given her food. She might have refused. I don't know what happened. I must admit, I did feel some happiness when I realized that someone could go so crazy about me. But what was I going to do with her? I wondered if I could go away somewhere else with her and try to make a life together. But it is hard enough for me to fend for myself. How could I take responsibility for another person? I look for a woman when I need some warmth. When I am done, I send the woman away. That is how it works for me. And since she came to me that night, I took her in and slept with her. But as soon as it dawned the next day, I took her and left her at her place. Then I took off on my own—a trip far out of town. My idea was not to return for six months. But I am not able to work like I used to. I am not feeling too well these days. So I returned just after a month. Upon my return, the farmhand said, "That woman comes once a day and asks when you are expected back." I tried my best to hide and stay away from her. But it is just a single field, and there's not much scope to hide. And so she came back.'

Once again, her husband and sons dragged her to her parents' village. Her natal family told everyone in the village that she had lost her mind. They had a few coconut trees in their field. They tied her to one of those trees. Not some flimsy tether. They did it the way it was done in olden days—making sure she could not move much. They also chained both her legs together and attached a large iron ball to the chain. It was very heavy. She would have to carry the iron weight in her hand simply to be able to walk a few steps. They fed her right there like they would feed a dog. Soon, she had blisters on her feet, which were wet with traces of sepsis. It was then that they took pity on her and untied her. After a couple of days, when her wounds had healed a little, she ran away again. People started saying that Nallayyan had resorted to some black magic by which he held control over her. Eventually, they found her again and took her to the foothills of Sellimalai, to Veppoor, to perform magic spells to counter Nallayyan's. But there was absolutely no change in her.

That was when they resorted to threatening Nallayyan. 'Whatever black magic you have used on her, you better make sure you end it now! Otherwise, we will kill you.'

'I have done nothing of that sort,' Nallayyan had tried to explain. 'Why would I? I have any number of women at my beck and call. Why should I covet your wife?'

But they refused to believe it. Now, Nallayyan ate what the farmhand cooked, then went away to wander elsewhere and returned quietly at night without anyone noticing. There was something menacing in the way his brother's sons looked at him. He was afraid that they would indeed kill him. They might smash his head with a rock while he slept. Once, when he was within earshot, one of his nephews had apparently said to the other, 'Get me that sickle, will you?'

After listening to this story, Seerayi said, 'I cannot understand how a woman could be like this. Everyone in the village says she has gone mad. I had gone there the other day to inform people about the meeting. I saw her then. She sat with her back against the wall and kept glaring at me like a woman possessed. Even I thought she had gone mad. And after listening to you, I too have my suspicions about you. Tell me, did you mix anything in the food you gave her? How else could she end up this way?'

'Why would I do anything like that, sister-in-law?' countered Nallayyan. 'I have seen quite a bit of life in all these years, but I have never met a woman like her. She has clearly gone over the edge. They will either kill her—or me. If they kill her, they will lose her and also not get the property they covet. If they kill me, this issue will come to an end and they will also have my share of the property. That must be their calculation. I don't know what to do. I am so worried.'

Seerayi scared him further, saying, 'Somehow, you have managed to wreck a family that was doing well. Who knows how many homes you have wrecked? All those bad deeds are hounding you now. They won't leave you in peace, you wait and see.'

He said, 'Please place your hand on your chest and speak truthfully. What did I do wrong here? He sent his wife to me, trying to take away my share of family wealth.

You don't seem to find fault with him for that. You are blaming me alone. Sadly, this is how the world works . . . I will sell my property and go elsewhere and live off that money. Or else, I will lease the land and earn some money in the bargain. Later, the property can go to whoever can pay back that money and reclaim it. Either way, I cannot stay in this village any longer. I need to go away. Let me see. There is a lawyer in Karattur. I am thinking of consulting him. I need to find out if the temple will feed me if I gift my land to the temple. Apparently, the white men are thinking of going away, giving us our lands back. They are saying that the laws will change after that. Let us wait and see. There has to be a solution to this.'

'Why suffer like this? If you had got married like everyone else, would you have come to this situation, running and hiding from everyone?' Seerayi sighed.

'Had Kali been here, he would have protected me,' said Nallayyan. 'But he is no more. I will seek refuge here if things become dangerous for me. Please don't forbid me from coming here. If you do, you might have to chop down a branch of the portia tree for me, just like you had to do for Kali.' And he laughed out loud.

'Earlier, you criticized Kali for his decision,' said Vallayi, coming out of her silence. 'And now you are saying you will do what he did!'

'Why would I kill myself, akka? If they come to kill me, I will make sure I kill at least one of them before I die. I am always carrying a dagger right here on my waist. I am not easily frightened. Why should I take my own life? I have some ideas. I need to see which one of them will work. I am not a stupid person who cannot think of a way out of a difficulty. I didn't mean it when I said I'd die like Kali.' Like that, he kept on talking.

Meanwhile, Ponna entered the hut and lay down on the cot, her mind swarming with thoughts.

TWENTY-FOUR

Muthu served everyone panagam made with dried ginger and sweetened with karuppatti. Some drank a little in their small cups, while others poured more into their carriers, perhaps to take some home for the elderly and the children who could not come to the meeting. Muthu had anticipated this, so he had made an entire pot of panagam. He had also kept aside some karuppatti in the basket, and also two pots of water, just in case he needed to make more panagam. He had brought his wife from his village well before dawn and got everything ready. The meeting was to take place in an open space in front of the village temple. Stones had been laid under the neem tree. Everyone drank some panagam and sat waiting on these stones, gossiping.

The washerman had spread two white dhotis side by side, and the barber had placed coconuts and fruits on them. Ponna sat in a corner with the other women. Vallayi and Muthu's wife, Poovayi, sat next to her. Several women had gathered for the event. Apart from the people who had come on Seerayi's invitation, there were many others who had come uninvited, because they had not witnessed such a ceremony in a long time and were curious to know how it was conducted. Thorattu Paatti was there, sitting with her legs stretched out. She had made some remark about such a ritual happening two generations ago, and this had led to questions from the cluster of women as to who it was and what had happened. Washermen stood here and there, carrying flaming torches, and some people beckoned to them to light up the areas where the people were planning to sit, to see if those spots were clean.

Seerayi looked around to see who among the kinsmen had come to the meeting, noting with satisfaction that there were one or two representatives from nearly all the families she had called. Even Seerayi's two younger brothers were there. A lot of people had arrived from far away, so there was a good deal of greetings and chatter. But Seerayi noticed that Nallayyan was not there. She wondered if he had already left town—or, more worryingly, if his brother and nephews had acted upon their threats and beaten him up. But she calmed herself, hoping that nothing of that sort had happened.

The village headman—who had been standing about talking to various people and drinking panagam—now came to the front of the gathering, and asked, 'Has everyone had some panagam to drink?'

To this, Kannaan from Thekkankaadu replied in jest, 'Everyone has drunk panagam to their stomach's content, and they are all now looking for a place to pee. In a little while, the entire village square is going to stink.'

Kannaan was a young fellow, but he was known for his sarcasm. The village leader now said, 'Who was that? It sounds like we have another Nallayyan among us!'

Kannaan replied, 'Yes! I want to go with him to the markets and fairs and find a heifer, but I am not able to catch hold of him.'

Everyone laughed.

'Couldn't you find a heifer right here?' someone asked.

'Here they are all old and shrivelled,' responded Kannaan.

'There is one like him in every generation,' said the headman. 'But how come Nallayyan is not here? Seerayi, did you inform him about the meeting?'

But someone else replied for her, 'Yes, yes, he has been informed, but he might have gone out of town.'

Everyone now fondly thought of Nallayyan, muttering among themselves, 'These village meetings are fun only when he is here.'

Listening to all the light-hearted banter, Seerayi felt a little comforted. Things might go smoothly after all.

The headman now said, 'All right. Let us begin. I hope everyone knows what this meeting is for. This is a matter primarily to do with women. That is why we have a lot of women gathered here. Usually, it is not in our custom to invite women to our village meetings. But this meeting involves a ritual, and that is why everyone is here. This is a good, full crowd. I hope the matter will be settled to the satisfaction of the people involved.' Then he addressed the barber and said, 'You can get started now.'

Someone from the crowd said, 'If we let women come to the village meeting, they might reveal all the dirty secrets of the men here!'

'I was just speaking about the custom,' intoned the headman. 'Let us not dwell on other trivialities any further. All right, let's begin.'

Someone brought a flame torch close to the place where the dhoti had been laid on the ground. The barber took some cow dung and moulded it into the deity. He broke open a coconut and immersed it in a pitcher full of water. He then placed in front of the deity a bowl containing a ball of rice, and asked for Ponna to be brought to that spot. Once she came and stood in front of the deity, he asked her to dip her hand into the water in the pitcher and sprinkle it around the spot. After that, he gave her three little balls of red-coloured rice and asked her to wave each of them in a circle around the deity before throwing them in three different directions. When he asked her to face the gathering and pay her respects, she lifted her head slightly and brought her palms together in a sign of respect. He then told her to go sit to a side, and he started speaking in a loud voice.

'Saami,' he said, loud enough for everyone to be able to hear, 'my respects to this gathering of elders, younger folk as well as older and younger women. The reason we have called for this meeting is, three months and eight days ago, on the twenty-second day of the month of Maasi, on a Thursday, early in the morning, the son of Thangasami and Seerayi from Periyakkaadu and the husband of Ponnayi ended his own life. Three months after that, Ponnayi experienced severe retching and dizzy spells, and the village midwife felt her pulse and declared that she was with child. We are in the fourth month now. The calculation of the number might be wrong by ten or fifteen days, saami. Ponnayi now stands in front of the entire village to declare that the child growing inside her is very much her husband's, and that it is the fourth month now, and she has cast three balls of rice around the deity. The foetus growing inside her will take Kali's name. The sun and moon over us bear witness to this, saami. Kinsmen from the families have come here from near and far—uncles, brothers-in-law and all other relatives. They have all accepted that the foetus within Ponnayi is Kali's. Even those relatives who could not make it to the meeting today, who are from the village and from other villages, have accepted this fact. Therefore, this village too should accept it, saami.'

He then stepped back a little.

A voice from the crowd suddenly said, 'It would be nice if all women come and make such a declaration.'

Then Thorattu Paatti, the elder, retorted, 'Why don't all of you men come in front of the village and swear that you have slept only with your own wives?' This created some excited chatter among the women.

The village headman intervened immediately and said, 'The barber has not finished the ritual yet. So everyone keep quiet now. You can talk among yourselves once the meeting is over. This girl here has lost her husband, and she has not fully recovered from that yet. We should not hurt her in any way. So please be quiet.' He then looked at the barber and said, 'Why did you stop? Go ahead, continue.'

The man resumed speaking right away, 'Saami, no one should speak words of blame, words of suspicion, words of insinuation, words of insult against our Ponna.'

A voice from the crowd slyly said, 'Will the child be born in ten months?'

Nobody could determine whose voice it was. But the headman said, 'Isn't that how long it takes usually for a child to be born? Who questions that? When one person among us faces a difficult situation, it amounts to a difficulty for all of us. They did not have a child for twelve years into their marriage, and Kali killed himself. We now have to make sure no one casts any aspersions on his wife, Ponna. If anyone speaks any such words against her, and if it comes to our attention, they will be punished. A situation like this befalls a woman so very rarely. Somehow, it has occurred now in our times. No one should ever face such a situation in the future. All right, now the village has accepted it. We can all disperse now. Those who didn't get to drink panagam earlier can drink some now before you leave.' And with that he brought the meeting to a close.

The barber returned the wide plate to Ponna after taking the fruits and coconut from it. He then said, 'Please give me my payment.' Immediately, Muthu went to the village headman and gave him the required amount. The headman then divided it between the barber and the washerman. A portion of the crowd walked up to the panagam pot. Others drifted away, talking among themselves. Seerayi invited the visiting relatives to her house, requesting them to stay for the night. Food had been cooked for all the relatives. Seerayi walked towards her house with all those relatives who had decided to stay the night.

Ponna had not lifted her head up the entire time.

TWENTY-FIVE

Ponna slowly adjusted to the natural rhythms of the changes occurring in her body. She was now able to deal with the myriad ways in which she felt every day: the difficulty she experienced getting up in the morning; the dullness and stupor that engulfed her even after she did manage to get up; and the dizziness and groundlessness and the need for stability that her body felt—everything. She dealt with each of these symptoms in its own way, without getting anxious. Now that Vengayi was coming in to work every day, Ponna even told her mother that she could go home. But her mother decided to stay put until the period of mourning was over.

Each of the four women had their own set of tasks every day. Vallayi took charge of cooking, washing dishes, fetching water from the well and other such household chores, and she did them at her own steady pace. Seerayi took the cattle out for grazing, tied them out in the pasture and fetched grass for their feed. She brought one bundle every day without fail. Some days, if she found other edible creepers and varieties of grass, she would bring another bundle. The rest of her time was spent herding the sheep.

Ponna supervised Vengayi's work in the fields. Only now, after all these years, was Ponna really getting the knack of all this work in the fields. In the twelve years since she got married and came over to live here, this place had been under Kali's control. Whenever she would go over to the fields, she would primarily engage in those tasks that she took pleasure in. Or else, she would carry out the specific chores that Kali had given her. But now it felt like she was getting used to everything afresh. Each time she gained proficiency in a particular task, she felt as though Kali had risen before her, as tall as a palmyra tree, and was smiling at her. She simplified some tasks to suit her pace. She asked Vengayi to place two large-mouthed earthen pots near the well. Each of those could hold two usual pots of water. If one could draw water from the well and fill these large pots, the bullocks would be able to drink water right there. Since they were taken to graze in the uncultivated field and the space between the other fields nearby, this would be a convenient spot to give them water. Otherwise, fetching water from this well all the way to the barnyard would be a massive task. Perhaps they might be able to carry two or three pots of water at the most. But after that, it would become far too exhausting. When Kali had been around, the very first things he did in the morning had been to clear away the cattle refuse and then bring water from the well. But only he could work at that efficient speed and pace. Ponna had also placed a large vessel for water near the weir, so that it too could be filled with the water drawn directly from the well. She even kept a mug nearby so that they could wash themselves right there. Usually, the three women at the farmstead would bathe only at dusk. But even if they had wanted to bathe during the day, there would have been no problem since there were no men around.

Ponna also set aside a separate pot that Vengayi could use to carry water. The issue was that Vengayi was not allowed to draw water from the well. But if someone else drew water, she could carry it in pots and fill the tubs in the barnyard. Whenever they used the picotah to irrigate from the well, all these various pots and tubs could be filled. In this way, Ponna came up with ways to make these chores easier. She was wonderstruck now, realizing just how many pots of water Kali must have drawn from the well every single day. And he had never complained about it. Perhaps it had not felt like a big task to him. She also set the sheep enclosure out closer to the fields but in such a way that they could still keep an eye on it from the barnyard. She let out the dog on a chain leash and tethered it right outside the sheepfold. She had already told Sengaan to bring a puppy which they could raise in the barnyard. But dogs usually got pregnant in the month of Purattasi and gave birth to their litters later. They would have to wait till then.

Since they had planted something or other in all the fields, she could not shift the cattle floor any further. And the task of cleaning the floor fell to Vengayi. Maize was growing lush in the fields. In just three months, once the maize was harvested, they could shift the cattle anywhere they wanted. It looked like they were all going to live mainly in the barnyard for a while. If they moved to the house in the village, who would watch over the cattle and the sheep? Ponna thought of living in the barnyard as akin to being nestled in Kali's embrace. She felt that she could not bring herself to be away from this place. They could use the house in the village to store utensils, dry pulses, big pots and so on. And they could go there once a month to sweep and clean the place. The hut in the barnyard had no wall. Kali had used it as a storage space. Now if they planned to live there, they'd need a wall around it.

Ponna thought it might be a good idea to build another shed where they could store additional things. The next time Muthu came around, Ponna talked to him about it—the first time she had spoken to Muthu since Kali's death. He had come to irrigate the brinjal bed and to see when they could sow ragi. By the time he had finished with his tasks, it had grown dark. So Ponna said to her mother, 'Ask my brother to stay here for the night. There is some more work to do. He can leave in the morning.' Her mother was delighted to hear her say that. And so was Muthu.

Muthu brought the bullocks back from the field and tied them up for the night. He kept fodder ready for them by pulling out stover from the bundles. Whatever was left over after the cattle had eaten, he piled up aside. Kali had never wasted even these leftover scraps of cattle feed. He would dry the leftover grass in the sun and then bundle them up. Cows munched on them in the summer. Muthu found it impossible to avoid thinking of Kali while working in the barnyard—each and every little task would prompt some memory or other. He wondered how Ponna was managing. Muthu cursed himself from time to time for ruining their little love nest. Now, after having completed all his tasks for the day, he sat down on the cot and ate his dinner. Vallayi had cooked a little extra rice than she usually made for Ponna. She had also cooked some horse gram. And since she knew Muthu liked it spicy, she had added an extra chilli pepper to the mix. Usually, Muthu never kept quiet while eating. He always had some opinion to offer—a word of praise or some complaint. But today, he finished eating in silence. Ponna emerged right then from the hut as if she had just been waiting for him to finish his dinner. It was very dark. They could sense each other's movements, but it was the kind of darkness in which they could not see each other's face clearly.

'We need to build a wall for this hut,' she began, without addressing him in particular, as if she was making a general remark. 'Only then can we really stay here. Apart from that, all we need is a little shed in a corner of the barnyard. We can store the spade, crowbar and all those implements there. It will be nice if you can find someone to get those things done.'

'We can get that done,' he replied. 'But why suffer this hardship? There are still six or seven months for the child to be born. You could go live back home in the village for about seven or nine months after that. I can come regularly and take care of the field and the cattle during that time.'

'I am not going anywhere. He might be dead for other people. But not for me. He is right here in this barnyard and in the field. He is watching over everything that I am doing, and he is right here with me. Even now, he is sitting on the portia tree and staring at me. I can see just his two eyes shining down at me like stars in the sky. I will do the tasks I can manage to do. If I am not able to do something, I am sure he will show up in some form to help me. Just like he sent Vengayi to help me out. I am only happy when I am with him. I know I will suffer terribly if I go anywhere else.'

Muthu did not say anything in response. He sat silently, looking down. Then he said, 'I will bring thatched panels and everything else that we will need. To build a wall, we need bricks and riverbed sand. I will bring these on the cart in multiple trips.'

Ponna said nothing. She simply went into the hut and lay down. Muthu could not sleep. And none of them knew at what time he eventually left. The next morning, Ponna glanced around the barnyard. Other than the rocks they used to weigh down the cattle fodder, she saw ten to twenty more lying strewn about here and there and by the fence. She asked Vengayi to pick these rocks up and keep them in the empty space behind the hut. It came to a small pile. If she could make three or four such piles, they would have enough rocks to lay the foundation for the wall.

There were some granite rocks lying in the area around the well. These were rocks that had been dug out of the well long ago. Kali had used some of these rocks to dam the water flowing from the weir to the water channel. Whichever of those stones could be lifted up, Ponna made sure they were brought to the pile behind the hut. As she walked around the fields, her eyes picked out the rocks that could be of use. On the field boundaries, by the fence, along the water channel—everywhere, rocks presented themselves to her. They had been lying right there all this while, but she had not noticed them before. Only when we become conscious of something does it make itself visible to us. Until then, even if it is right in front of us, we would never become aware of its existence. Ponna was amazed at the various shapes of the rocks she found. Mostly, she found black granite and a kind of quartz. But she also found a few riverbed rocks that could break easily.

The common path that ran by the field was a long one. It started in the village and went past so many people's fields to who knew where. It perhaps went all the way to other villages. Maybe, it ended at the hillock in Mavoor. Ponna suddenly felt that she should walk along that pathway one day. 'Where does this path lead, Venga?' she asked.

'It lies stretched out like a cobra, Ponnu,' she answered. 'I have not walked a great distance on it. But it has to end somewhere, doesn't it?'

Ponna asked her, with the excitement of a child, 'Shall we take that path to the end one day?'

'Why not?' said Vengayi. 'Let us pack some food and leave at dawn one day. And let us walk until dusk. I don't think the path could be longer than that. Then, if we find some village where the path ends, we could spend the night there and come back in the morning.'

Ponna liked that plan. She really wanted to go along that path to see where it led. It was wide enough for carts to travel on. In the sowing season, carts constantly moved up and down that path. And then once again in the harvest season. On either side, it had short trees and bushes. If she looked along that path, she might find innumerable rocks. But she asked Vengayi to look, cautioning her to stay close to the path and not venture into the bushes. She also told her to pick only those rocks that she could carry.

When they were done with their work in the field, they walked over to the path to pick out more rocks. There could be scorpions or centipedes underneath, so they were careful to always roll the rocks over first. If there was nothing under it, they would claim that rock. But if they found any creature nestled below, they would let it run away before taking away the rock. Once, when they rolled over a particular rock, the red scorpion that lived under it got crushed to death. The baby scorpions that had been in its belly scattered and ran everywhere. There must have been about twenty of them.

'Oh no,' lamented Vengayi, 'the scorpion died.'

'Baby scorpions always come out tearing open their mother's belly,' said Ponna. 'Some creatures die once they propagate their species. The scorpion too is like that. So don't worry. Look how there are ten to twenty baby scorpions now. Out of these, at least five or six will survive.'

And so the two of them continued gathering the rocks along the path. After a while, it looked like they might have also collected enough rocks for the new storage shed they planned to build. Ponna even considered the idea of building a wall for that shed too.

It also occurred to her that Kali had been just like that red scorpion—dying as it gave birth to its offspring.

TWENTY-SIX

Once the period of mourning was over, Ponna became even more active.

She paid attention to every single change in her body, hoping that she would soon regain control over it. Now and then, she would touch and feel her belly. She'd press down a little with her hand but would soon release it, worrying it might hurt the foetus. She had been told that she would be able to sense its movements only after the fifth month. She was very eager to experience that moment, to know how it felt. As of now, she just found everything new and a source of wonderment. Even Vengayi noticed this new sense of excitement in Ponna. The day the period of mourning ended, Ponna's mother and mother-in-law cleaned and mopped the house thoroughly. Her brother, Muthu, and her father went to the hill temple. Initially, they wondered if they should invite some of the kinsmen to go along with them, but that would have meant going personally to call on all the seventeen families of kinsmen—and so Ponna decided against it and asked just Muthu and her father to go to the temple.

However, since they were not supposed to go in twos, it was decided that Muthu's son would also accompany them. They first offered prayers at the foot of the hillock, then went up and made offerings there as well. Once they climbed down, they also stopped at the temple at the base and made offerings there. The womenfolk went only to the village temple, where they had given money to the priests to conduct an abhisekam, a ritual bath, for the deity. They made sweet pongal for the goddess and offered it along with coconuts and fruits, making sure they gave enough to please the deity. Ponna had fervently prayed, 'I want my husband to be with me always. Please don't send him away. I want him to be happy. I want every little thing I do to make him happy. Please make sure he does not suffer.'

The very next day, Muthu fetched a man to help them build walls for the hut in the barnyard. Looking at the stones piled up, the man remarked, 'It looks as though there are enough stones here to build an entire house!' They decided to build a proper wall, using both stones and sand. Muthu suggested that they build the new shed first and then perhaps turn it into living quarters. But Ponna did not agree. It was this hut in the barnyard that had been Kali's space. So, she said, this was where she would live. Everyone tried pointing out that Kali had spent time in the entire barnyard, so why not build a new hut and live there instead, but Ponna refused to agree. Muthu did not want to pressure her, but he was still determined to build the new shed well, with sturdy walls and a thatched roof good enough for them to live in. He also asked the worker to divide the space into two and then construct a separating wall inside. He said that if they built the new structure first, they could move all their things into it for safekeeping during the rainy season which would be starting soon. Ponna had the final say in all these decisions.

Seerayi usually had suggestions to offer. But seeing Ponna's firmness in her decisions, she remarked, 'This is all yours from now on. Your work, your responsibility, your fields, your house. You do what you want. I just need to while away the rest of the years that are left with me.' So she did not interfere in how things got done.

Even after the construction of the walls began, Ponna continued to go looking for stones with Vengayi. It made her happy to venture out and traverse that path. She also went to the southern corner of the fields, where she had ceremoniously placed a rock over Kali's buried ashes, and just stood there solemnly. Then, one day, she asked for some stones to be brought to that spot. The palai sapling she had planted there had grown a little. She cleared the spot around the plant and arranged the stones in a circle, making a little bed for the plant. Then she placed a flat stone in front of the rock, which for her had become a sacred rock.

Seerayi wondered what Ponna was up to in the fields for quite so long. After two days spent in speculation, she went over to the spot to see for herself. Looking at what Ponna had done, she sat down and started crying. 'It is not in our custom to plant a rock in someone's memory,' she said, raising her voice in anguish. 'Please don't start new practices and bring ruin to this family!'

Ponna said, 'Atthai, this is a temple for Kooli.'

'You are not supposed to have a temple for the goddess Kooli in the fields, my girl,' said Seerayi. 'She is a fiery one, she will destroy everything.'

'This is for Kooliyappan, Atthai,' Ponna clarified.

'Kooliyamma or Kooliyappan, it doesn't matter—they are both aspects of the same goddess. Please listen to me. Don't do this. People only have Karunchaami in their fields. And our fields did not have even that. Apparently, we had a deity a long time ago; but when the lands were divided among people, that portion when to someone else. I have heard that even after that, our family still went to that other plot of land to make pongal offerings for the deity, but after some family feuds, that practice too came to an end. Since then, we have had no deities here. Why are you starting something new now?'

'This *is* Kaattu Karunchaami, Atthai,' answered Ponna immediately. 'All other fields have one. Kali used to say that we needed to have one too. We couldn't do it when he was alive. So I am doing it now.'

'In our community,' said Vengayi, 'we have the practice of planting a rock in memory of a dead person. Every year, when we celebrate Pongal, we make offerings for these shrines. Those who are dead are the same as gods, aren't they?'

And that was that. From then on, Ponna told everyone it was a shrine for Kaattu Karunchaami, the deity protecting the fields, that only he could ensure good crops, that they should light a lamp for him there every day, and that in the month of Thaii, they should offer pongal and sacrifice a rooster to the god. To some, she even said that the deity had come in her dream and said, 'If there is no temple for me, how can I keep an eye on the crops? Build me a shrine, light a lamp.' Sometimes, she remarked that the reason for all their misfortunes was the fact that they did not build a shrine for Karunchaami as soon as the lands had been divided. And those people who had already built their own Karunchaami shrines after they inherited separate fields tended to agree with her.

After the period of mourning was over, Vallayi had left for her village. Now it was Ponna who mostly did the cooking. One day, Seerayi brought the sheep back from grazing, shut them up in the enclosure and went all the way to Vallayi's village to speak to her. 'It is true that she is a know-it-all,' she said, 'but this is too much. There are times when she seems to be doing fine, but at other times, she acts like a possessed woman. I don't know how to deal with this.'

The next day, Vallayi came over, making it seem like a casual visit. After looking at the new shrine, she asked Ponna about it. And Ponna gave her a story, like the ones she had been telling everyone else. It was only ten days ago that they had sowed ragi and planted chillies. Ponna now told Vallayi that all the ragi they had planted had gone pale and withered and so she had prayed to Karunchaami, who had then appeared in her dream and said, 'You have not given even a little space for me in your fields, have you? Since back when your husband was alive, I have been wandering as the wind, struggling to find a little dwelling space for myself here. Find me a resting spot. I will make sure your ragi grows lush and healthy.'

Vallayi did not say anything in response. In fact, when she saw the shrine, Vallayi felt it was a good thing. There was a shrine to Karunchaami in everyone's field, so what was there to lose by offering him a little space in a corner here? And if Ponna thought of it as a memorial for Kali, that was all right too. So she said to Seerayi, 'Don't worry, Seerayi. Let it be. She thinks of her husband as a god. It is rare to come across such women these days, isn't it? We both know of women who did not wait for long after their husbands died before shifting their attentions to other men. And here we have someone who worships her husband. It is a good thing. Let her be. Remember in what state she was before this. We thought she too might end her life on the portia tree. She has come a long way since. She takes care of all the farming work responsibly. You don't worry about anything. Just do your work and try to be at peace.'

Ponna sent word to her brother through her mother, asking him to bring a lamp cage. And so he brought her one the next time he visited her in order to irrigate the ragi and the chillies. The potters in Kannur had made varieties of lamp cages that year. Many people were in the habit of making pongal offerings for Karunchaami in the month of Aippasi. At that time, they would replace the old lamp cages with new ones. You could buy a new cage in exchange for two measures of kambu millets. The one Muthu brought had been painted in ochre and had white stripes over it. With its raised and pointy top, it looked beautiful. Ponna placed it next to Karunchaami. Muthu was astounded when he looked at the shrine. She had laid flat stones and made a proper floor for it. He felt that once the palai plant grew into a tree, this would be an incredible spot. He stood in front of the deity and prayed, 'Ayya, saami, please forgive me if I have done you wrong. Please don't punish me for what I did unknowingly. Come and inhabit this spot. Let Ponna give birth to the child and live well. Next year, I will offer you a sheep.' He also told Ponna what he had promised the deity.

Muthu had still not gathered the courage to look Ponna in the eye when he spoke to her. He spoke to her as if he was addressing Seerayi. But hearing of Muthu's entreaty to Karunchaami made Ponna very happy. The same day, she asked Seerayi, Muthu and Vengayi to come to the shrine for a special ceremony. She lit an earthen lamp with castor oil and prayed to Karunchaami. She asked the others to pray too. She also lit some camphor on the flat stone she had placed right in front of the deity. When all of them returned to the barnyard that night after this prayer, they felt contented.

Ponna felt a new excitement, as though all her happiness had now finally been restored.

TWENTY-SEVEN

The brinjal plants had grown big and fully taken over the bed on which they had been planted. Good, big vegetables. Each brinjal was the size of a cat's head. Ponna cooked them in a variety of ways. One day, she cooked them with coconut, adding just a little water. She used four brinjals for that dish. They were bright green, and they retained their colour even after being cooked. Ponna and Seerayi had enough to eat for all three meals that day. Another day, Ponna mashed the brinjals with some tomatoes, and added some ghee which gave the meal an exquisite fragrance. Yet another day, it was brinjal roasted over the fire and reduced to its essence. Then there was brinjal ground into a paste and cooked with some tamarind. And brinjal with thuvarai lentils. And brinjal with black-eyed peas. They had brinjal every day, but cooked in such a way that they never got tired of it. It was only now that Seerayi was getting to see Ponna's cooking skills. She was no longer surprised at how enchanted Kali had been with Ponna.

There were so many brinjals that Vengayi could take two home every day. Ponna also sent some to her parents. Seerayi plucked the rest of them, sold them at the Tuesday market and bought other household things with that money. Ponna went and spoke to each brinjal plant every day. If she saw even a single wilting leaf on any of those plants, she immediately plucked it away and buried it in the sand. If she saw any insects or worms on the plant, she crushed them to death. Aphids preyed on the underside of the leaves. She had to be watchful of those. She wrapped the ashes from the firewood stove in a cloth, and sprinkled the ash over the brinjal bed, making sure it fell not only on top but also under the leaves. The brinjal bed was irrigated well, since the water from the intermittent rains had collected in the dug-out channel.

The chilli plants too thrived, with flowers and new fruits growing lush all over. Some of the chilli peppers had also ripened a little. They harvested the ripe ones and spread them to dry on a little rock out in the field. Seerayi estimated that they would harvest at least twenty measures of chilli peppers. If they dried them in the sun and then stored them in lidded baskets, they could sell them for a good price at the markets in the months of Chithirai and Vaigasi. That was Ponna's plan too. She was able to spot the chillies as they ripened. The ragi too had grown well and filled out the entire field. They would be able to harvest the sheaves soon. And since it was growing on only one enclosed field, they wouldn't need to hire extra help. Ponna could do the work with help from Seerayi and Vengayi. But they would have to make sure the rains of the Karthikai month did not wreck the harvest.

Both huts would be built by then, so they could store the harvest inside if need be. They could also cut the ragi stalks. But they would have to be dried before threshing. So it would be all right if they let the stalks stand for ten or fifteen days before harvesting them. They could do the reaping in the month of Margazhi. If they do that at the beginning of the month, they could use one of the beds to plant onions. And they could also plant some pumpkin and cucumber since they wouldn't need much water. Using the moisture in the soil, they'd grow and spread out. And after Margazhi, they could harvest maize. Ponna's plan was to get all of this done without hiring extra labour. If they did all of this properly, they wouldn't have much work to do after the month of Thaii. They'd only have to look after the cattle and the sheep.

As per Ponna's calculation, the child would be born sometime at the end of Margazhi or the beginning of Thaii. These days, she was able to feel the baby kicking inside her. In those moments, if she stood hunching, she felt the baby's movements comforting. From the force of the kicks, she wondered if it was a boy. Kali would want to be born as a boy. But why? Why not as a girl? Ponna really wanted a girl. Seerayi said that there was some curse that no girl child would be born in this family, and so firmly believed that it was going to be a boy. But Ponna prayed that a girl should be born, if only to put an end to that curse. Why should it be the fate of this family to have only male children who live short lives? 'Let it be a girl child and a new lineage that thrives in these fields,' she wished.

One morning early in the month of Karthikai, Ponna's family arrived in a bullock cart. It was a complete surprise for Ponna. Her brother, Muthu, had come just a few days before that and drawn water from the well to irrigate the fields. Usually, he never sent Sengaan for these tasks, but rather came over himself to do the needful. This way, he had a chance to see Ponna regularly. He'd keep his gaze on the portia tree or on Seerayi while asking after Ponna's health. Ponna found this amusing, but she never replied to these queries herself. Only Seerayi did. Muthu was a loving brother, that was why he was suffering this way. He'd go spend a little time at the Karunchaami shrine. He'd pray there, sit for a while. He took that as a chance to talk to Kali.

Both huts had had their walls built by then, and Muthu had made sure their roofs were properly thatched. Over these roofs, he had ragi sheaves spread close and tied tight. This way, the roof would stand for ten years. Kali had kept aside a pile of unthreshed ragi sheaves. The cattle wouldn't munch on them. Muthu also had a similar pile back home. He had used both these piles on the thatched roof. The new shed was quite big, and Seerayi had started using that space a lot. Doors had been fixed for both huts. But at night, Seerayi still slept outside the hut where Ponna slept.

Even Seerayi had not told Ponna that her family was arriving that day. All sorts of gifts came in their bullock cart. It was the ninth month of Ponna's pregnancy. If Kali had been alive, they would have thrown a feast for the entire village and taken Ponna back home with them with all fanfare. But that was not possible under the circumstances. Also, if they had expressed their wish to come and treat Ponna to a feast, they knew she would object. That was why they came without telling her in advance. Seerayi was immensely happy about all this. She had wanted this for Ponna, but she had not known how to talk to her about this. Ponna never went anywhere beyond the barnyard and the fields. Vengayi and Seerayi were her only sources of contact with the outside world. If someone from the village paid a visit, Ponna chatted with them. Also, Thorattu Paatti and Noni Kizhavi, two elderly women from the village, paid a visit at least once a week. Ponna always listened eagerly to their chatter, but she never spoke much herself.

The two elderly women advised her on what she could eat. If she had any doubts, she asked them. Out of Ponna's earshot, they said to Seerayi, 'If your son was alive, the in-laws would come to throw a feast and pack food for their way back home with Ponna. Unfortunately, given the circumstances, that is not to be.' But what could Seerayi say in response to that? Ponna too thought about it, but she did not feel like a feast at this point. It was kind enough of them to come and visit regularly. She had heard that Muthu was telling everyone: 'You should see the way

Ponna runs the farm affairs there. Even a man can't work so efficiently.' She felt satisfied just hearing that. But when the entire family showed up one morning in the bullock cart, she did not know what to say. She said gently to her sister-in-law, Poovayi, 'What was the need for all this? You have brought all these gifts as if all was well and I am giving birth to this child in happiness.'

'It does not matter, Ponna,' said Poovayi. 'The very fact that you are having a child is cause for happiness.' And then she carried on with her work.

Muthu and Ponna's father went over to the fields. Vengayi was removing grass from the water channels. Muthu said to her laughingly, 'Are you and your landlady done with the task of picking stones?'

Vengayi laughed too. 'No, saami. We are still picking them out and piling them up here. She says she wants to build a stone wall all around the fields like a fortress.'

Ponna's father said, 'I won't be surprised if you do it.'

They felt a certain contentment as they walked around the fields. And when they returned to the barnyard, some spicy vadai awaited them, ready to be eaten. And not just that—there were rice cakes too, and three varieties of rice dishes: tamarind rice, tomato rice and curd rice. Ponna had planted a plantain next to the spot where they washed their hands. They took leaves from that tree to use as plates.

Ponna's face looked pale, and there was some swelling in her feet. Her mother said to her, 'Ponnu, you need to take better care of your health. If you carry on like this, you won't even have the energy to push the child out. Just come home with us. We will cook whatever you want to eat. You can have a good, safe delivery and then return here.' Poovayi echoed the same sentiments. Ponna did not say anything in response, but her smile conveyed to them that she was not going to leave this place. Her eyes were fixed on the portia tree. The place where they had cut the branch from the tree had gone dark, and mushrooms had sprouted there. In her heart, Ponna felt sad that Kali was not alive to enjoy the feast. But she took little portions of each of the dishes made, and placed them on a tile she had kept on the kizhuvai tree behind the hut. She always kept a handful there of whatever food she made. Some crows always came to eat that food. On that day too the crows came. Only after she heard the crows did she help herself to some food.

Vallayi asked her, 'All right, then shall I come and stay here with you? If you need something in the night, your mother-in-law may not be able to handle things on her own.'

Ponna said to her, 'It is enough if you come in the month of Margazhi. Vengayi is here in the afternoons. At night, a few old women come over and stay here talking until it dawns the next day. There is nothing to worry about. The midwife too comes. We have also told the midwife not to travel too far from the village. She says the moment the belly stops dropping, she will be able to tell when the baby will be born.'

That day, Ponna's family left only at dusk. Ponna gave Vengayi portions from the various dishes cooked that day. 'Take these for your children. Tell me one thing. You have given birth to three children. So tell me honestly, does it hurt a lot while giving birth?'

Vengayi laughed, saying, 'It will hurt, yes, but it won't hurt a lot.'

How much was the difference between hurting and hurting a lot?

TWENTY-EIGHT

Once the month of Margazhi began, Ponna stopped going to the fields. She confined herself to the barnyard. She had a view of the fields from there, but there was not really much to see. Everything just lay spread about. The leaves on the brinjal plants had ripened to a rich yellow. As for the chilli plants, only the stalks remained. All the harvesting had been done and the produce was safely kept in the house. 'It is your turn now,' Ponna said often, placing her hand over her stomach. These days, she had started panting even if she walked a little distance. But then, she was also not able to just sit around doing nothing. She needed to engage herself in some task. So she continued to do all the cooking.

Seerayi too was active. Once she finished cleaning the floor of the cattle shed, she took the cattle out and left them tethered in the pasture for grazing. And once she stepped out of the barnyard for a particular task, she also got other things done, like gathering and bringing back a bundle of dried leaves of the castor bean plant. The sheep liked to eat the leaves of this plant when they ripened and fell. Seerayi brought these in little bundles and piled them up. In the months of Panguni and Chithirai, when the sun would scorch and dry out the pastures, they could feed these leaves to the sheep who would eat with relish without wasting a single leaf.

From the barnyard, Ponna had a clear view of the shrine. As per her instructions, Vengayi brought more stones and stacked them around the shrine. On its east side, the shrine now had a stone wall that was nearly waist high. Ponna told Vengayi that once the wall was completed on three sides, they must have an arched entrance built on the front side.

The palai plant had now grown quite tall. Next to it, a neem tree was coming up on its own. She had asked them to let it grow and not cut it down. If both grew into big trees, they would cast a lovely shade over the shrine. That year, she did not offer pongal at the shrine. Everyone told her to do it the next year onward, once the child was born. And she agreed to that. But she went every evening without fail and lit a lamp at the shrine. She carried a cup of oil and walked to the shrine at that time of the evening when the day had ended but some of its light still lingered like a shadow. Seerayi ranted to Vengayi, 'Lighting the lamp every day requires pots and pots of oil. Even that may not be enough. Do you think we can afford that? Why can't she light the lamp every Friday and on special occasions? Has anyone ever lit the lamp for Karunchaami every day?

There are people who think of the deity only when they are offering pongal, and they go look for him in the overgrown grass and behind the rocks only then. But here she has built a proper temple for him.' However, she never said anything directly to Ponna.

The midwife placed her hand on Ponna's belly and told her that the child would be born in fifteen days, and since the belly was quite big and Ponna had some difficulty breathing, she said it must be a boy. But she added, 'They say even god cannot predict the blessing of rain and child. We just make educated guesses with the symptoms we observe.' Ponna's mind was on the midwife's words while she made dosai using ragi batter in which some karuppatti had been mixed. She made two dosais for Seerayi and two for herself. And as she sat on the flat stone outside the hut, eating the dosais, she heard Nallayyan's voice. She also heard another voice, a woman's. Seerayi grew apprehensive, wondering if Nallayyan was bringing one of his women there. It was indeed a woman who came with Nallayyan, but it was only Thorattu Paatti from the village.

Seerayi said to the old woman, 'You could have come earlier when there was still some daylight, couldn't you? Why are you coming now in the dark? If you trip and fall somewhere, who will answer your grandchildren?'

Thorattu Paatti walked over and sat down on the cot, replying, 'Well, if I fall, I will hopefully just die. But death does not seem to come so quickly for me.'

And Seerayi said, 'It wouldn't be a problem if you die as soon as you fall down. But if you break an arm or a leg, who will care for you? Who will clean up your pee and shit?'

'That's true,' agreed Thorattu Paatti.

'Paatti, where did you find Uncle?' Ponna interjected, turning their attention towards Nallayyan. 'I thought he had left the country and gone away for good.'

Seerayi addressed him now and said, 'That's right, brother-in-law. I haven't seen you in six months. I wondered if your brother carried out his threat and killed and buried you in the ragi fields. I asked him about you a couple of times when I ran into him. He only said, "That motherfucker must be roaming around somewhere, up to no good, that wretched dog!" How could I respond to that!'

Thorattu Paatti now expressed her doubts. 'Whenever I ask them about your brother's wife, they say she is still at her parents' village. But I wondered if you took her with you when you ran away from here. Apparently, these days, people are even marrying outside their caste—and then they run to the big cities and try to make a life there.'

Nallayyan laughed. 'You old women! Here you are in the countryside, gazing at crows and sparrows, but you actually know a lot about what is happening in the outside world. If someone's wife and someone's husband get together, do you think the village lets them be? So they have to leave, even if it means sailing away across the ocean. I think if two people fit well with each other, like mortar and pestle, people should just let them be. But I am not young any more—am I?—to run away with a woman and start a new life somewhere. Even when I was young, I was too lazy to do any hard work. There is no way I can take on the responsibility to feed and take care of a woman.'

Then he told them what had happened. He said he had grown very fearful living in his own house. Even if he heard the sound of a lizard running, he wondered if it was his brother and nephews coming to attack him; he would look through the gap between the doors to make sure. He had travelled so much, spent time in various places with all sorts of people, but he had never experienced this kind of fear before, he said. How long could he live in fear? So the very next day, he sold off his cattle and sheep. He gave some money to his farmhand, and let him go. Then he went away. He was returning now after six months.

'Before I went away,' he said, 'I had sowed maize in my field. I don't know what they did, whether they let it be grazed to death or if they harvested it and kept it all for themselves. Now there is not a sheaf to be spotted in the field. The borders are broken, the fields are barren, and they have left it lying like a cremation ground. It may not be their land, but they are farmers too, aren't they? Don't they know this is not how you treat a field, no matter whose it is? You may not like a person, but you cannot take it out on their land.'

Paatti responded, 'It is hard enough to take care of one's own fields. What do you expect? You just dropped everything and ran away, and you expect others to take good care of your field and keep it in perfect shape? You can't blame anyone. Especially if you were not willing to labour hard and work the fields yourself. Anyway, where were you these six months?'

Never before had Nallayyan had a problem finding someplace to go. But this time, he said, he could not figure out where to go. He spent a night at a rest house on the way to Mangoor. A group of mendicants were staying there, and he learnt from them that they were undertaking a pilgrimage to a hundred and eight temples. He joined them. They walked long distances every day. When they couldn't walk any further, they would take shelter in a public rest house or some such place. And whatever food they got in their begging bowls, they shared and ate. If they got any kambu or ragi grains as alms, they sold them in the markets. Whenever they arrived at a temple, they got at least one free meal. The only thing they did not sell, but safely put away, was the rice they got in alms. On days they did not find any food from their usual sources, they cooked and ate the rice.

Nallayyan said, 'We needed very little. An ochre-coloured dhoti and a towel. And an alms bowl. That was all. If we held the bowl in front of people, they dropped something into it without turning us away. There were even people who fell at our feet for blessings, you know. This was how I survived for six months. How many temples we visited! All of us have only been to the temple in Karattur, and we think that is a big temple. You should go to the temples in the Chola country. Those kings have built such massive temples, each one taking up several acres. People there tell you that such-and-such a king built this one and so-and-so king built that one, and so on. Also, in those parts, people don't eat the kind of nonsense we eat here, all this kambu meal, ragi gruel, samai meal. They eat only sparkling-white paddy rice. Even a day labourer eats rice there! In these six months, I learnt a new way to make a living. All I need to do is push my alms bowl towards people. I can fill my stomach.'

Hearing all this made Thorattu Paatti very angry. She asked, 'You are born to a farmer. How can you beg for your food? And you call that a living? Nallayyan, in our community, we might go hungry and tie a wet cloth over our tummies to suppress the feeling of hunger, but we don't accept food we have not worked for and earned. Did your mother really bear you for a farmer?' Ponna felt very uncomfortable at this turn in the conversation. She quietly removed herself from there and went and lay down inside the hut. But she could still hear their voices.

'How do I know whom my mother slept with to give birth to me?' quipped Nallayyan. 'It is possible that even she didn't know. Let's say a woman sleeps with ten men. Will she be able to tell which one of them is the father of the child she gives birth to? Also, do all farmers conduct their lives the way you have just described? There are men in this caste who send their own wives to other men.' His rage mounted as he spoke further. 'Taking to the alms bowl is not an easy task. You need to be able to beg, hold your hand out to ask. Do you think it is easy to get used to that? If a man starts thinking about the fact that he is a farmer, that he has land and fields, that he has come from a good family, and that all this is beneath him, he cannot bring himself to beg. He has to cast away all that. He has to understand that he is nothing, that he is not as significant as even a strand of hair. And these other things like pride, honour, shame, respect, prestige, relatives, wealth, comfort—he has to shed everything. That's the fact. People are all the same. We can hold our hand out to beg from anyone. We can accept food from anyone. Who are you? What have you accomplished on this earth? You have tilled the land all your life, but what have you got to show for it? Your entire life has gone by. And it is the land that is going to consume you. Now, it is going to be ten months since Kali died. Not even his bones remain. Then why do you have this meaningless pride? Will you be able to give up everything? It is a big thing to do. Only a really exalted person will be able to do that. I tried to give up everything, but I couldn't. I still have all sorts of useless stuff in my heart and mind. I don't know when I can sweep all of them away for good.'

'What has happened to him?' murmured Seerayi. 'Why does he speak like a fool?'

TWENTY-NINE

Nallayyan continued with his story. Apparently, his youngest brother's wife then went to live with her eldest daughter in Ookkur, about ten miles from Aattur. They had canal irrigation in those parts, so there was a lot of work to do in the fields. But she ran away from there two or three times and came looking for Nallayyan. Seeing how bereft his house and cattle shed looked, and how dusty and littered it was, she wept. The farmhand was not there, so she had no way of finding out what had happened. Her husband and sons then chased her away, and she walked all the way back to her daughter's home in Ookkur. So now, if Nallayyan went to live in his own house, she might get wind of that and come running to him again. But Nallayyan seemed not to be thinking much about her.

'I regret taking my share of the inheritance,' he mused. 'This is the only thing that ties me down now. I am unable to just let go of everything. Nor am I able to make a living with it. I am really confused. Selling it off does not sound like a practical solution. I have three and a quarter acres. It will fetch me about seven hundred rupees. But where will I keep that money? I cannot carry it as I wander around, can I? I sleep on the roadside, I sleep in rest houses, sometimes I sleep under tamarind trees. Will I be able to sleep if I carry that much money on me wherever I go? Moreover, if I start spending the money even little by little, how long will it last? If I get too used to having cash in my hand and spending it at will, then that will spoil me. One option is to lend it and live on the interest it fetches. But whom do I see about that? Everyone wants money, but later they might completely deny that they took any money from you. What do I do? Tell me, sister-in-law! Sometimes I think I should just bestow it upon these wretched dogs. If I die, run over by a vehicle, people might consider me an orphan and simply do away with my corpse. But if I continue to live and suffer various ailments before I die, only if I have a little money would anyone be willing to care for me. I don't know what to do.'

Thorattu Paatti said, 'This is exactly why one needs a family. Does a family man have to worry about these things, tell me? I don't have any children. I have no wealth in my name. After my husband died, I came to live at my brother's home. At that time, my in-laws gave me fifty rupees. I kept it for myself. To this day, I have spent my time doing whatever work I can do. Now my brother has a son and a grandson, and it is this grandson who feeds me nowadays. I still do whatever work I am able to do. If I did not have a family, do you think I would have managed to survive? Tell me, Nallayyan.'

'Paatti, an old woman, carries thousands of rupees in her little waist purse,' said Seerayi. 'You are a man. And you are crying about keeping seven hundred rupees on you!'

Thorattu Paatti added, 'I don't have any money. I lent those fifty rupees I had here and there over the years, and I have added some five or ten more to it. That is all. One of these days, when they bury me, I don't want people to say, "That old hag had absolutely nothing."'

'Family and all that won't work out for me, aaya,' said Nallayyan. 'I am a free bird. I find food and water on the go and I figure out life on a day-to-day basis. If nothing at all works out, perhaps I could leave this world like Kali did. I made it very clear to my brothers yesterday. I said to them, "I am now used to carrying the alms bowl. I can do that even here in our own village. I have no shame about it. But I am thinking about how it would reflect on you two. Also, there are people willing to take my fields on lease. It needs to be watered every three days. And each time, it will irrigate about four sections of land. It is red soil. So whatever you sow will grow. There is also a house and the cattle shed. A full family can move in. What do you say? I suggest you two split the lease and keep the harvest. I don't need any produce from the fields. Just give me cash. I don't want to lease it out to strangers. But you should give me the money at the beginning of the year. Do this, and I will write this land over to you in my will." They have said they will think about it. The youngest brother wants me to lease it out entirely to him. He was the one who sent his wife to me. But I am somewhat scared of dealing with him. And if I do, then I should have witnesses from the village present. The only thing is that the villagers will then ask why we are involving them only now and how come we did not consult them earlier.'

Listening to all of this made Ponna very sad. Never before had Nallayyan spoken in this manner. He always engaged in happy banter. But then again, no one's life stays on the same course. Something or other comes up and steers us in a different direction. It is not up to us to decide our paths. Suddenly, Ponna realized that Nallayyan had made several references to food. So she asked him, 'Maama, have you eaten?'

He said, 'Oh, Ponna, no, I have not eaten anything. I thought I could eat something here. But just as I arrived, I saw you and your mother-in-law finishing your dinner and washing your hands. And I didn't want to saddle a very pregnant woman with additional chores, so I kept quiet. But unmindful of our convictions, the stomach makes its need felt. You somehow figured that out. If you have some water-soaked rice, please give that to me. I will try to quieten my stomach for a while.'

'You are a strange fellow!' said Seerayi. 'If you had told me you were hungry, I'd have given you something to eat.'

Ponna walked out of the hut, laughing, and said, 'You could not even ask *us* for food. So how were you planning to beg for food from strangers?'

Nallayyan laughed and said, 'It is easier to ask strangers.'

Instead of giving him water-soaked leftovers to eat, Ponna mixed some ragi flour with water and onions and chillies, and made spicy dosais for him. This was no big task for her. She also made one for Thorattu Paatti, who praised Ponna: 'I don't know how you learnt to cook so well. The brinjal you cooked the other day was so fragrant. And now this dosai, it is so tasty, Ponna. Someone has to make bangles to adorn your precious hands.'

But Paatti realized the mistake of her remark when Ponna replied, 'No more bangles for my hands, no chains for my neck, no earrings for these ears . . . But I appreciate the sentiment, aaya.'

Immediately, Thorattu Paatti tried to salvage the situation by saying, 'It does not matter if you can't wear any of that. Don't worry. Even women who get to wear all these things still have to leave this world naked when they go.'

Nallayyan, meanwhile, ate with relish. 'Ragi flour is perfect for dosai. So much better than making a pap from it.' Ponna made another dosai for him, this time sweetening it with whatever karuppatti was left from their dinner earlier. It was very satisfying to feed him. And it looked like a full stomach had also made him happy, as was evident from the buoyant lilt in his speech. 'Let me come and stay here in this barnyard and eat what you feed me,' he said. 'I will bequeath my property to Ponna. What do you say, sister-in-law?'

'Do that!' encouraged Thorattu Patti. 'This way you will also be ensured a place to live.'

But Seerayi said, 'I don't think such an arrangement will work out, Nallayyan.'

Ponna felt that there was a tentative desire in Seerayi's tone. She sat down on a stone and spoke to him. 'Uncle,' she began, 'we don't need any inheritance. If we work hard in these fields, we can make enough to feed two more families. Already, people in the village have all sorts of things to say about us. If we accept your money, they will have even more fodder to be nasty. They will easily say that I was your mistress and that was why my husband killed himself. I know that you were very fond of my husband, but do the others know that? We have to adjust to the village's norms. If those norms require me to stand in front of everyone and declare that this child in my womb is indeed my husband's, then I have to do that. What else can any of us do? We have nowhere else to go. Besides, we are womenfolk. We can't fight with your brothers. Even you are afraid of them and are hiding here and there. If they come to hack us to death, are we strong enough to fight them off? If we accept your money, it will destroy our peace. How long can we live on without peace, tell me? Visit us once in a while. We will cook and feed you whatever we can. Even stay a while with us. But let us not talk about money and inheritance. I am already enduring the misery of having lost my husband. I don't need to add to that suffering, do I, Maama?'

There was a pause as the roaring wind pushing the portia tree ceased.

THIRTY

On the first Thursday of the month of Thaii, early in the morning, Ponna gave birth to a boy. No one had any doubts that it was Kali himself who was born as this child. Every known relative visited to see the baby. And they all said the child resembled Kali. But for a month after giving birth, Ponna could not stop weeping. She was unable to discern what it was that made her cry—whether it was because the baby was a boy while she wanted a girl, or because she was afraid that this male child might also end up having his life cut short. Ponna was still weak from the childbirth. Seerayi always asked her to go to bed early each night. Seerayi and Vallayi did all the work—carrying the baby, bathing him, massaging him with oil and so on. They also did their best to help Ponna gain strength, by making all sorts of nutritious things for her to eat and drink.

Ponna had struggled a lot during the labour and delivery. Vengayi had earlier told her that it would be a little difficult. But there was nothing 'little' about it.

A slight pain had started the day before, but Ponna did not realize it was the onset of labour. She had earlier had this kind of sharp pain in the hip and her lower abdomen sometimes in the morning, and they always went away after a short while. So she assumed it was a similar sort of pain she was experiencing. But it only kept increasing in severity. By midday, when she could not bear it any longer, she told Vallayi about the pain. After asking Ponna to describe the pain, Vallayi told her with certainty that it had to do with labour. As the pain kept mounting, Ponna began to feel a little scared, and she sent Vengayi to fetch the midwife. Seerayi asked the farmhand from the adjacent fields to go to Adaiyur. By the time the midwife got all her things ready and came over, it was past dusk. Until then, Ponna kept asking when the midwife would arrive, as if she thought that once the midwife got there, she would take over the pain from her.

When Thangayi, the midwife, arrived, she did not seem to be in any hurry. She felt Ponna's stomach and said that the child would be born by morning. Ponna was shocked to hear that. She had thought that once Thangayi showed up, the birth would take place right away. Now she was terrified thinking she had to bear this excruciating pain all night long. Vengayi left, saying she would go home and return soon. Seerayi went to tie up the cattle in the shed. Thangayi said, 'Ponna, don't worry. Since this is your first child, there will be some pain. But enduring this pain will not be as hard as you fear. You have survived all kinds of struggles and heartbreaks. What can this pain possibly do to you? Remember, this is the good kind of pain. It will lead to good things.' She told Ponna not to eat anything until the delivery. She also advised her to make sure to defecate beforehand.

She gave Ponna a karuppatti concoction to drink. She had brought a lot of things in a box. But she did not take any of it out just yet. Then she too left for the night, and it was only Ponna and Vallayi. Ponna felt like everyone had abandoned her. Before she went to the outback to shit, she went to the Karunchaami shrine. But she was not able to pray at leisure. Holding on to her aching hip, she prayed, 'Please make it all go well.' She could not think of anything else to say.

When she returned home, she drank a little of the karuppatti concoction and lay down on the cot. But she could not stay in that position for more than a few seconds. She sat up, turned to the other side and lay down, but this was not any better either. She got up and walked outside the hut. As she sat down on the rock there, she started crying.

Looking at her crying, Vallayi said, laughing, 'You can cry, but it is still you who have to give birth.'

Ponna replied angrily, 'How can you laugh when I am crying?'

Her mother said, 'If you can't bear even this pain, how are you going to manage? You are yet to have contractions. Once that happens, the child will be born soon. That will feel like your entire hip is breaking apart. You will have to endure that.'

Now slowly, one by one, several people landed up. Soon there was quite a crowd gathered in the barnyard. The midwife too returned. She gave Ponna some medicinal brew in a pitcher and asked her to drink up the entire thing. It was bitter and pungent, but Ponna hoped that drinking that would decrease her agony or perhaps increase the pain and let it all be over and done with soon. She drank it up in one gulp, but nothing happened. Some of the people who had showed up started dispersing, saying to each other, 'Looks like the child will be born only in the morning.' Those who stayed back chatted and laughed among themselves. Some lay down here and there. Ponna was irritated by all this. The midwife would ask her about the pain now and then. But then she too went to sleep.

Ponna couldn't tell what time it was when she dozed off. Nor could she say how long she might have slept. She felt both rested and yet not. Very early in the morning, Thangayi gave her another dose of the medicinal brew. By the time the black drongo birds started making their ruckus at dawn in the palm trees, Ponna's pain intensified. Unable to bear the agony, she screamed, 'Ayyo! Ayyo!' The midwife said to her, 'Don't say "Ayyo!" Say "Saami!" Say god's name.' Once the contractions started and her water broke, the midwife asked her to lie down and then told her to push. Ponna held her breath and pushed hard. Thangayi pressed on her abdomen firmly. But these measures were not enough. So the midwife asked for a thick rope to be brought and suspended from the central beam on the ceiling. Muthu came in to do this task, and he walked away without even turning to look at Ponna. Two or three women held Ponna and helped her off the cot. Then they brought her to where the rope was and asked her to hold on to it. Ponna kept her feet apart, knelt down and held on to the ends of the rope. It felt to her like the rope was hanging from the portia tree.

She closed her eyes, pulled against the rope and pushed hard. Just one push—and she felt her breath ending and something giving way in her stomach. Then she fainted, vaguely hearing someone say, 'It is a boy.'

Later, when she came to, she saw everyone wandering about happily. She heard her sister-in-law's voice: 'This boy is exactly like his father, Ponna. So utterly dark.' Ponna did not have the strength for a good cry; she just managed to whimper. Her sister-in-law showed her the baby, but Ponna did not take a good look. Even later, Ponna did not look at the child properly.

For a month afterwards, her mother and mother-in-law did everything for the baby. Ponna slowly started eating properly. She was able to walk on her own to the outfields to relieve herself. Her mother told her that it was a month since the child was born and so that was the day they would show a lamp to the child. Vallayi was busy preparing things for this occasion. She poured into a large earthen lamp the fresh castor oil they had got made by sending castor seeds to the oil press. Then she put in a thick wick and placed the lamp on its wooden base. Seerayi came into the hut. Ponna was sitting on the cot.

Positioning the lamp in such a way that the child would be able to see the flame from the cot, Vallayi lit the lamp. As the wick slowly caught the flame, a yellowish glow pervaded the entire room. Seerayi gently tapped on the baby's cheeks, trying to get him to open his eyes, and said, 'Look here, dear one.' The baby slowly opened its eyes, and then blinked, adjusting to the glare of the light. Then it looked in wonder at the dancing flame. That was the first wondrous thing in the world the child laid its eyes on: that flame. The two women talked to the baby for a little while and then went away to prepare things to ritually ward off the evil eye.

Ponna saw the movement of the flame and the movements of the baby's eyes. She suddenly felt very eager to look at the child properly. The baby's eyes slid back and forth between her face and the flame. She happily ran her hands over the baby's unruly hair and its dark body. She felt a rush of love and fondness for her son that she had not felt until then. She massaged the baby's legs, placed its little hands on her cheeks. She looked at the baby's penis; it looked like another finger. She said, 'Little penis!' and kissed her fingers after they had touched the baby's penis. The baby now kicked its legs and burbled something to her. Ponna started cooing and playing with the baby. She gently touched its belly, and placed her face close to the baby's.

The baby looked up in wide-eyed wonder at her face growing bigger as she brought it nearer, and then becoming smaller again as she pulled back. After she did that four or five times continuously, the baby laughed. It opened its mouth wide in a gurgling laugh. Ponna was delighted. As she reached out with her fingers to touch the baby's lips, she heard a voice say, 'Tell me if this is a big mouth.'

Did the baby just say that?

She looked at the baby's face, and suddenly she recollected that face and that voice. That face that she had met on the eighteenth day of the festival. The face that had asked her, 'Do I have a big mouth?'

That face that was buried deep in Ponna's mind.

THIRTY-ONE

He had spotted Ponna as she stood alone in the midst of the swirling crowds. Then she too spotted him.

He gave her a name of his own: Selvi. She did not need a name for him. There had been a massive crowd on that festival day; various acts and performances were being staged on the streets. When they saw the two of them together, many people whistled and hooted at them. Ponna kept her head lowered as she walked. He held her hand and led her away from the crowd very quickly. They both walked in the glow of the moonlight that was dispelling the darkness all around the temple rock. Now he had his arm around her waist, pulling her closer to him. She regarded his embrace as his way of helping her get rid of her fear. She huddled closer to him.

His appearance and physique were very much like Kali's. Around his waist, he wore a veshti folded twice over itself. On his bare chest, he just had a towel draped around his neck. And a big piece of cloth covered his head. Ponna thought that this was perhaps his way of concealing his true identity. Kali too wore his veshti in two layers whenever he went out. And a towel over his chest. Sometimes he would take that towel and wear it over his head. When it brushed against her like this, Kali's body too was hard like a granite rock. She shook her head to get Kali out of her mind. This man was not Kali. Why was she projecting Kali's image on to him? This was a different man. This was the god himself who had come to take her someplace else. Hesitantly, she placed her hand on his waist. He pulled that hand closer and positioned it firmly. Where was he taking her? She was not able to recognize that road. There were a few people walking down that road, but it was mostly quiet and secluded, with nothing but moonlight illuminating it.

Suddenly, he turned and walked towards the rock. At least, that was how it appeared to her. She did not know there was a pathway there. There were only rocks there, she had thought. He took her there. He climbed up on the rock with the easy agility of a goat. Sometimes, he let her walk with him, and at other times, when the path became precariously uneven, he gently lifted her and helped her across. It looked like they had climbed a quarter of the hill. There was a large rock standing upright over there, and behind this feature, the rock was as flat as a floor. They could only see the moon above. There was no one else. He removed the cloth he had tied over his head. It was neither a towel nor a dhoti, it was of the size of a dupatta. He spread it on the ground, sat down on it and invited her to sit down too. As she sat down, he pulled her against his chest. She yielded to him, tempted to encircle her hands around his back. And his hands held hers and gently guided her in an embrace.

The moon travelled across the sky, spreading joy over the world. Not a spot of cloud dotted the vastness above. With nothing to block its path, the moon gloriously shone across the heavens and over the earth. The land that drank the moon's sweet rays lay about in a drunken stupor. A sprawling expanse of intoxication.

Then he asked her, 'Did you come seeking a child?'

She did not reply, but just placed her face on his chest.

'You will have one,' he said. He caressed her lips. 'You won't talk?'

But her hands spoke.

'Will you name the child after me?' he asked.

She softly murmured, 'Hmm,' in his ear.

Then he said, 'Whether it is a boy or a girl, you should name the child after me, will you?' He felt her nodding in agreement on his chest. 'My name is . . .' he said. 'Tell me, what did I say my name was?'

And like she had done before, she whispered in his ear, '. . .'

He said, 'You voice feels like moonlight spilling into my ears.'

Then he lifted her face in his hands and, bringing it level with his, said, 'I have another name too,' and laughed. 'Look, when I laugh, my mouth appears big, doesn't it?

Look and tell me if I have a big mouth—am I an aalavaayan, one with a wide mouth? Tell me.' He opened his mouth wide. It was indeed big. But how could she tell him that. He sensed her laughing a little.

'It is big, isn't it? That is why in my village I have a nick name: Aalavaayan. Do I have a big mouth? Tell me. Am I Aalavaayan? If it is a boy, name him Aalavaayan. If it is a girl, name her Aalavaaychi. Will you?'

Ponna could not help but laugh at that name.

'You are laughing? Do you know what all a big mouth can do?' And then he pulled her face towards him. Once again, she felt the coolness of the moonlight. 'Do you know which village I am from?' he asked. She placed her hand over his mouth to show she did not want to know. He said, 'Don't worry. I am from this very hill.'

He went on, 'You should come next year too. With the child. I will be expecting you. Will you? You will. I know you will. You won't forget me. Even if you forget me, I won't be able to forget you. Do you want to go away with me? Tell me. I will just take you with me. I like you very much. Why don't you come with me?'

His words kept growing until they fell like blank noise in Ponna's ears.

THIRTY-TWO

Ponna looked over and again at the baby's mouth. It was big. A big mouth. Aalavaay . . . And there *was* a resemblance.

The baby now closed its mouth and looked at the flame, enraptured, before turning its gaze back to Ponna. This way of communicating with silence—that was Kali's face.

Her mother and mother-in-law came into the hut and warded off the evil eye from the infant.

Seerayi said, 'Look at how intently it is looking at the lamp! What do you see there, darling?'

Vallayi said, 'He has his father's face.'

In the one month since the baby was born, how many times had people made that remark! Every visitor had said the same thing. But Ponna alone saw another face in the baby's expression. And that face said to her, 'You should come and see me.' It will be Vaigasi in just a month. And this year, apparently, the chariot festival was scheduled for the very beginning of Vaigasi. Perhaps she could go and see that face again?

That face would definitely wait for her. It would firmly believe that Selvi would come. Would it recognize her in the white sari? It will. It will hold Selvi's hand. But what would she tell Kali? Kali's face was an illusion, wasn't it? But despite being illusory, it still appeared in front of her, clear and full of life. And she kept explaining herself to it every day. Now both faces appeared alternately in front of her, laughing. She could not fall asleep even late into the night. But later, when sleep finally overtook her, she would not even hear the baby crying. Her mother woke her up, saying, 'When you have an infant, you can't sleep like this.' Ponna did not even hear her mother clearly. She went about breastfeeding the baby as if by reflex.

When the baby placed its mouth on her nipples, she closed her eyes. Which mouth was this? Kali had small, pouty lips. The other man had a big mouth. Which one was this? It felt like a little mouth sucking with a big one. She felt Kali's hunger in its rapid feeding. She switched breasts. It looked like the baby had had enough milk. It was teasing her nipple with its lips. This was Kali teasing. The baby dozed off with one of her nipples still in its mouth. She lay the baby on the cot and gently wiped some milk from its mouth. The baby then closed its mouth. Whose lips were these? Ponna stepped outside the hut.

It had been long since dawn. Why did she feel so muddled? Her gaze fell on the portia tree. She looked askance at its magnificent form. It had spread like a giant umbrella over the entire barnyard. It was not going to leave even a tiny space uncovered. It would keep spreading its branches in all directions. Losing that one branch had increased its vigour. In the ten months since Kali's death, it had thrived, with leaves and twigs and branches extending further and further. For the first time ever, she tried imagining what the place would look like if the entire tree was felled and removed. If it became just a plain expanse, she could plant a fresh stalk. Or she could just let it be a sun-drenched space. But even after she felled the tree in her mind, it returned and stood firm. She used all her energy to cast it away from her mind. But it stood immovable. The tree was not out there on that spot, it was in her mind—in that place where neither saw nor axe could remove it.

Asking her mother to watch over the baby, Ponna went out to the field. The stones they had placed around the shrine shone in the light of the early-morning sun. The rock she had planted had firmly claimed its place. She had planted it and nourished it with blood. It could not be removed now. Lamp ceremonies and pongal offerings would take place here from now on. Once in a while, it would demand a blood sacrifice. 'Can't you help me live without suffering?' she asked. She did not know what else to ask. Then she returned to the enclosure.

She felt like something was shadowing her, but there was nothing. 'Yes, this is how you fool me,' she said. The baby was still asleep. She sat down on the rock outside the hut and drank the dry-ginger concoction her mother had given her. This was supposed to ensure the child didn't catch a cold.

One day, her mother said, 'Ponna, it's been three months now. Let us go to our village and stay there for a couple of days. Your mother-in-law says we can also name the child while we are there. What shall we name him?'

Seerayi, who was near the cattle floor, said, 'This is god's child. We have to name him Maachaami, after the deity. But if we name him that, the entire village will come to know. We won't be able to explain it to everyone. So let us give him that name but call him by a different one. Some twenty or so years from now, when it is time for him to get married, we can say that his real name is Maachaami. Who is going to question us then? There is nothing wrong in having two names, one for the house and one for the world. We have a thousand names even for god. So why not for a man?'

The baby made a sound. Ponna ran inside the hut to check. It was awake and it laughed at her, kicking its tiny feet in the air. Then it burbled in its own baby language.

'What is your name?' she cooed. 'All right, I will call you Kannu, my little calf, my little treasure.' The baby laughed, opening its mouth wide. 'I am going to give you another name. But you shouldn't tell anyone, all right? Aalavaaya, the wide-mouthed one—hey, Aalavaaya!' She whispered this secretly and lay down close to the baby, embracing it to her chest.

Ponna found great joy in that embrace.

GLOSSARY

aaya: grandmothers or women of that stature

kizhavi: old woman; a more casual way to refer to an elderly woman

maama: how women of certain communities address their husbands; also the same kin term for maternal uncles

mapillai: literally, son-in-law; also a mode of affectionate address towards men who have married, or could potentially marry, a woman from one's kin group

nangai: a regional kinship term for sister-in-law

paatti: grandmother or anyone who is considered to be of that stature and worthy of respect

saami: a word with a complex set of social usages—as a term of endearment, as a mode of address marking caste-based hierarchical relationships, as a word for a religious deity, etc.